CUPIDS BOW RANCH

A Montana Country Inn Romance Novel - Book 1

AMY RAFFERTY

Formatted by Author Services by Sarah

STAY UPDATED WITH ME

Thank you so much for purchasing or downloading my book! I am grateful to all my amazing readers.

To stay updated on all my latest books, newsletters, freebies and beautiful photos from the fabulous locations I write about, why not join my VIP group?

I will send you regular pictures of La Jolla Cove, San Diego and the Florida Gulf Beaches where I try to spend as much time as I can. I live in San Diego, my own 'Garden Of Eden' and I am in love with the sea and the beaches in the area. They inspire me to write lots of beachy mystery romance fiction to share with my awesome readers like you. To join me go to https://landing.mailerlite.com/webforms/landing/y6w2d2

You will be asked for your email. You also get a FREE BOOK whenever you sign-up!

FREE BOOK

To get your FREE copy of Cody Bay Inn Prequel - Nantucket Calling go to www.amazon.com/B0992NFTY1

CHARACTER LIST

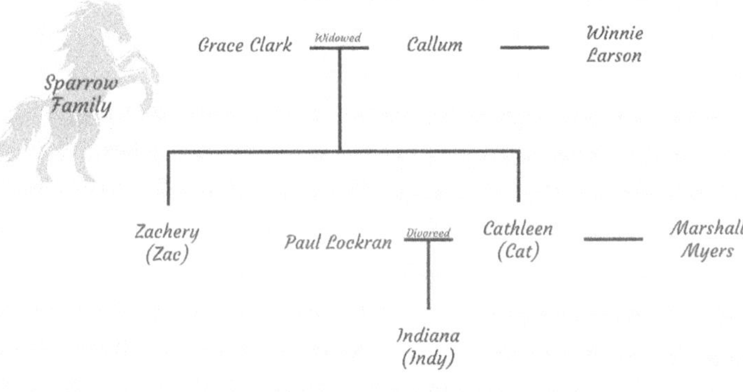

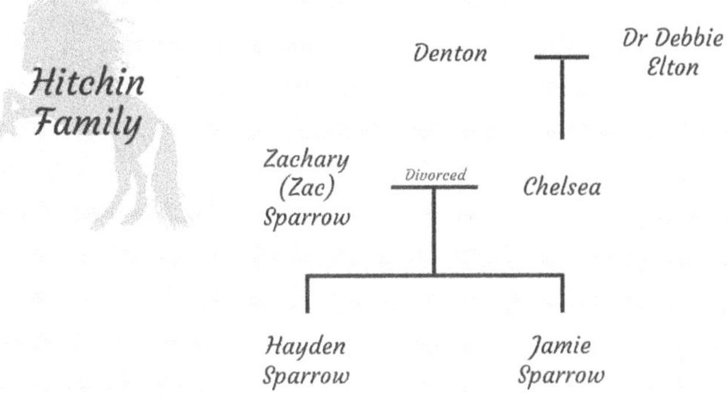

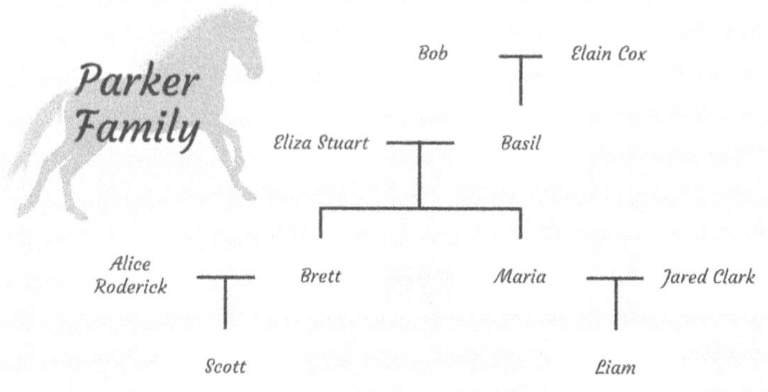
Parker Family
Bob
Elain Cox
Eliza Stuart
Basil
Alice Roderick
Brett
Maria
Jared Clark
Scott
Liam

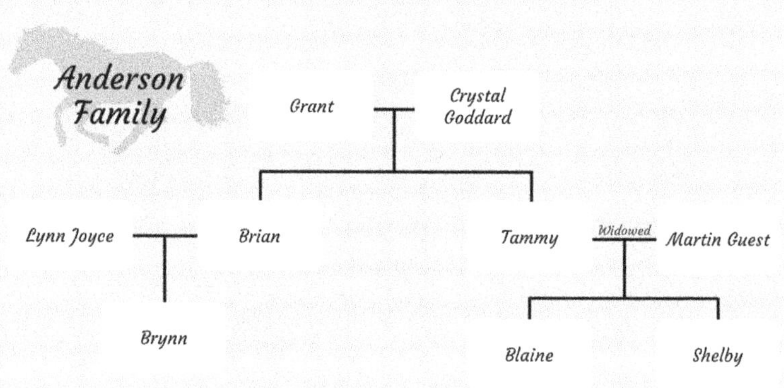
Anderson Family
Grant
Crystal Goddard
Lynn Joyce
Brian
Tammy
Widowed
Martin Guest
Brynn
Blaine
Shelby

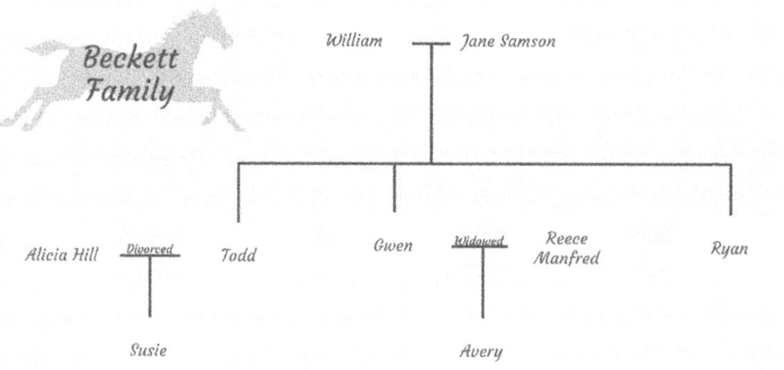
Beckett Family
William
Jane Samson
Alicia Hill
Divorced
Todd
Gwen
Widowed
Reece Manfred
Ryan
Susie
Avery

MAP OF THE RANCHES

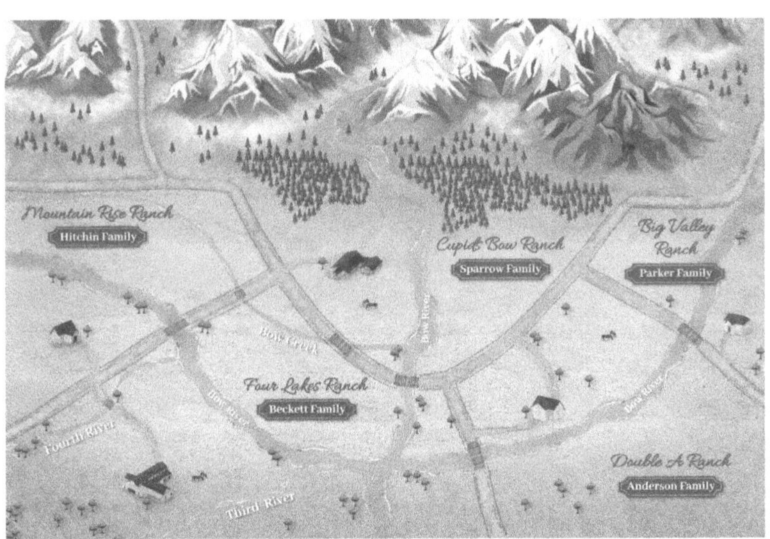

PROLOGUE

BEFORE THE SERIES BEGINS

HAVE YOU READ Restless Hearts Beneath the Big Sky, the prequel to the Montana Country Inn Romance Series?

To read the prequel for FREE, go to www.amazon.com/dp/B09W6BB899

People born in the big cities, where skyscrapers block out the skies above and dull the stars at night, all scatter to the country.

They are all desperate for a breath of fresh air, hoping to find direction in the stars again. As for those born and raised in the country, their hearts long for the glitter and glamor the big cities promise. But what if the grass isn't always greener on the other side?

Growing up in a small town, you soon run out of new people to meet, and the chances of a big romance with a stranger or a career are few and far between. Then there are age-old family feuds that limit your options further! That is why the new generation of the Sparrow, Hitchin, Parker, Anderson, and Beckett families decide to head for the greener pastures of bigger cities in search of love, fame, and freedom. Until the land they call home needs them once more...

Nothing mends broken fences faster than uniting against a common enemy. But can these five families move through the hurt, anger, mistrust, and betrayal to fight for their future and save their family homes?

Find out in the Prequel to Amazon #1 Best Selling Author, Amy Rafferty's new Montana Country Inn series, set in the breathtaking wilds in the Big Sky country. Fall in love with unforgettable characters, who face sadness and life's challenges with bravery, love, and hope.

Chapter One

RETURN TO CUPIDS BOW RANCH - PART ONE

PRESENT DAY

Cat had been back in Montana for two days and she hadn't been to visit Cupids Bow Ranch or her older brother, Zac. Her son, Indy, was there at the moment and she knew she'd have to go see him. Now an architectural engineer, he was helping Cat's brother with some plans for a building expansion on the ranch. Cat hadn't seen Indy in the three months since her life had blown up and he'd come to Montana to help Zac.

Cat pulled the throw she had around her tighter as a cold brisk breeze tried to squeeze into the gaps. She pulled her feet up onto the chair and sipped her morning coffee. It was still early, and the sun had just started to climb up into the sky. Cat was sitting out on the balcony of her room at Big Valley Ranch. She was staying at the ranch as a guest of one of the owners, Maria. Cat stared out at the Big Snowy Mountains looming in the distance. She loved springtime in Montana.

Everything was beautiful, from the grass to the birds that came out of hiding as the snow slowly started to melt. Cat had grown to love Nashville, and she had an apartment in the city with a house in Brentwood. While the city was amazing, she had her mansion in Brentwood she'd retreat to after a long music tour. But often over the past thirty-one years, her heart had yearned for the freedom and wide-open plains of Montana.

Cat had missed her home terribly over the years and had used her homesick emotions to put the feeling and passion into her music. Although Cat hadn't set foot on Cupid's Bow Ranch since she'd left at the age of nineteen, she'd made sure her son got to meet her family. Indy had spent a lot of his summers with her brother and his cousins at Cupid's Bow ranch. Indy loved the ranch and had often begged to go live there when he was younger. Once he'd finished university, he'd jumped at the chance to go work at Cupid's Bow ranch.

Even Indy's father, Cat's first husband, movie star, and producer, Paul Lockran had fallen in love with Cupid's Bow Ranch. He too had often backed Indy up about them moving back to Montana as a family. Maybe if she had moved back to Montana with her family back then she and Paul would still be married. Then Cat wouldn't be in the bad predicament she was currently hiding from out in Montana. Cat sighed, thinking about her first marriage. Paul had been one of Cat's first great loves. She'd thought they'd had the perfect marriage. So did their fans. Cat Sparrow, one of the top country singing stars, and Hollywood heartthrob Paul Lockran were said to be an inspiration to every married couple. Well, that turned out to be a bit of a joke, although only Cat and Paul knew what really happened to their marriage.

Paul had always been so attentive and loving. He always held her hand or had his arm around her and Indy couldn't have asked for a better father. Paul always did his best to make sure he was there for every milestone in Indy's life. He also did his best to be there for Cat. At all her concerts Paul could be at, if his filming schedule allowed, he and Indy would be in the front row wearing their Cat Sparrow's #1 Fan t-shirts. He proudly attended all her award ceremonies, and as far as Cat knew their love deepened every day. They had been labeled as the perfect showbiz couple.

Their twenty-fifth wedding anniversary had been plastered all over the papers and showbiz news sites. So, it had come as a huge shock to Cat to find out about Paul's long-term affair. It had been an even bigger shock to find out that the affair had been with Astrid Hove.

Astrid was an actress who played the part of Paul's on-screen wife in his long-running supernatural television show. She was also the wife of Paul's older brother, West Lockran, who was the owner of Lockran Talent Management and Cat's manager. Paul had broken both her heart and her trust in people. Especially after finding out just how many of the people who worked around her every day had known about the affair. Not only did she feel like her soul was bruised and her heart bleeding, but she also felt like a huge fool for not seeing what was right under her nose. After that big shock Cat realized that she may have actually known or suspected something all along, but had chosen to ignore it.

Cat shuddered and swallowed the tears that would still leak from her bruised soul whenever she thought about Paul's treachery. Poor Indy had been so angry with his father when he'd found out, that he'd refused to have anything to do with Paul. Indy hadn't spoken to or seen his father since the split, which was four years ago. Indy hadn't even attended Paul's second marriage a mere eight months after their divorce. Because both she and Paul had shiny reputations to protect, the affair had been hushed up. West's PR agency had done a sterling job of making sure nothing besmirched hers and Paul's shiny reputations.

To keep their fans happy and iron out any disappointment their split had caused them, Cat and Paul had to put on brave faces and pretend the split was mutual. As far as the world was concerned, she and Paul were the best of friends who'd simply fallen out of love. Cat should've won an Oscar for her performances when she had to appear in public with Paul and his new girlfriend. As soon as Cat and West had found out about Paul and Astrid, the couple had ended the affair. Paul hadn't wanted the divorce and he had begged Cat to forgive him. He wanted them to work through their differences because he still loved her. But she felt it was more about keeping his fans happy than wanting to patch up their marriage.

Up until Cat had found out about him cheating on her, she didn't think they'd had any differences to work out. She'd told Paul that if he'd loved her, he never would've cheated on her for the past five years. She'd known the world she worked in was a treacherous one, but Cat had thought herself lucky in her marriage and with the people she worked with. She had naively trusted them all. When Cat had found out that most of them knew about Paul's affair her first angry instinct was to fire her whole team. But instead, she got them all to sign a non-disclosure agreement which stated that if anyone leaked anything they would all be sued.

Her lawyer had written airtight contracts and if they refused to sign, Cat's PR agency had ready-to-go statements for the press about each one of them. She knew it was unethical and Cat hated having to do it. But she'd been good to each one of the people who worked on her team. From her cleaning crew to her make-up artists, set designers, camera crew, and so on. Cat made sure they got good bonuses. She knew nearly every one of her team's family and couldn't believe they'd not told her what was going on behind her back.

Cat's aunt, Simone Clark, who was a legend in the Country music business, had warned Cat not to get too close or friendly with anyone in their business. She said that at the end of the day it was a cutthroat business where everyone was just out for themselves. Cat hadn't wanted to believe that was true. She'd handpicked each one of her team of people who worked for her. But as it turned out, the only person she could trust had been her housekeeper, Ava. Paul and Astrid had kept their affair out of their homes until a few days after Cat and Paul's twenty-fifth wedding anniversary.

Cat had left for a music tour the day after the celebration. On the second day of the tour, she'd gotten a throat infection and had to cancel the tour. Cat had gone home to her house in

Brenton where she knew Paul was staying while the television show was on hiatus. She couldn't wait to see him but instead, she was greeted by nearly twenty calls from Ava. Cat never kept her phone on her while on tour. It was a distraction and emergencies went through either West or Cat's assistant. But the minute she turned her phone back on there was message after message from Ava.

When Cat called Ava back her housekeeper told her that Paul was there with Astrid. At first, Cat had thought that Astrid had come to visit. But when she got home, she realized that was not the case. Cat had caught Astrid and Paul together in the pool house. She'd picked up the phone and called West who was already on his way because Ava had called him too. It was a day Cat wished she could forget, but instead it was one of those wicked memories that loved to torment her at the most inappropriate times.

One year later, Paul married a new up-and-coming young rock star he'd met while on location for a film in the Bahamas. For appearance's sake and to keep up the ruse of a mutual split, Cat had to endure four days of Paul and his new wife's company when they met her on tour. No one ever got to know the truth of what Cat had gone through because of Paul's cheating or how the divorce had affected her. Except for Indy, she'd shut everyone else out and poured everything she had left inside into her music.

"Cat?" Maria Parker knocked on the bedroom door. She and her brother Brett had inherited Big Valley Ranch from their parents. "Can I come in? I know you're already awake."

"Of course," Cat called. "I'm out on the balcony."

"I know," Maria told her, walking towards the balcony with two steamy cups of coffee in her hand. "I was out riding the ranch just before sunup when I saw you out here." She put the cup on the table next to Cat. "I thought you might like a hotter, fresher cup. You've been hanging onto that one for ages."

"I've been sitting here watching the sun come up over the mountain thinking how much I've missed this view," Cat told her. "I remember when I was young. My two best friends and I would climb up to the loft in the old barn and watch the sun rise over the mountains."

"Did you make a wish each morning when you saw the first glint spark off the river?" Maria asked her. "I used to do that. I thought that glint was the sunbeams tickling the fairies awake and making them sprinkle their fairy dust into the air."

"Aww, that's the sweetest story," Cat said, grinning. "We would shout, good morning sun, as it peaked over the highest tip we could see. It was supposed to ensure we had the best day."

"Now I think that's sweet." Maria smiled, settling down on a chair next to Cat. She pulled a dollar from her pocket and put it on the table next to her. "There you go."

Cat laughed. The day Cat had left home thirty-one years ago was the same day twenty-year-old Maria Parker had decided to run away from home. Cat and her best friend Ashley Cuthbert were driving to Billings so Cat could catch an airplane to Nashville. Maria was also headed to the same place, wanting to catch an airplane to Nashville to go study there. Cat and Ashley had picked Maria up along the road where she was trying to hitch a ride. When they found they were both headed the same way they'd decided it had been fate.

Maria was a year older than Cat and Ashley. Although they knew each other because their ranches shared a border, they had never really been friends. But their adventure to Nashville together had changed that and turned them into best friends. Cat had invited Maria to stay with her at her aunt Simone Clark's place in Nashville. Simone had taken both Maria and Cat under her wing to teach them how to fly as close to the sun as possible. And both herself and Maria had done just that. They'd become extremely successful in their chosen careers. Cat as a country singer and Maria as a talent agent. Maria had also married Cat's cousin, Simone's son Jared Clark and had a son, Liam, together. Liam and Indy were only a year apart in age and had grown up like brothers.

"Maybe I should give you another dollar?" Maria laughed.

"You look like your thoughts are a lot more than a dollar's worth today."

"I've just been going for a few trips down memory lane." Cat sighed, putting down her cold coffee to pick up the fresh mug Maria had brought her. "This is a lot better, thank you."

"You're welcome," Maria said, taking a sip of her coffee. "I hope you're not wasting your thoughts on that two-bit scoundrel who's trying to ruin your life."

"No, I wasn't thinking about Marshall," Cat said with another shudder. "I was thinking about Paul."

"Agh!" It was Maria's turn to shudder. "Another two-bit scoundrel that doesn't deserve a second thought." Her voice was laced with anger. "This morning when I saw the first sun glint, I wished you'd find a man worthy of that big heart and gentle soul of yours, Kitty Cat."

Tears sprang to Cat's eyes at Maria's words. "Thank you," Cat said softly, reaching out and giving Maria's hand a squeeze. "But I think you should rather be saving your wishes for a good man deserving of you and all that love you have to give them."

"Now, you're going to make me cry," Maria told Cat, her eyes misting over. "I don't want to start this glorious day off with tears."

"No, but I do need you to take me into town to go see Ashley," Cat said. "She's handling all my legal work for me now."

"I'm so glad you fired that shark of a lawyer you had in Nashville." Maria took a sip of her coffee and pulled her legs up onto the chair.

"I had to, as he was still Paul's lawyer," Cat explained. "It wasn't right, and I didn't feel comfortable with it."

"No, neither would I," Maria agreed. "I've been meaning to tell you that I've handed Simone's estate over to Ashley to handle for us as well."

"Of course," Cat said. "I told you I'm more than happy for you to handle it any way you thought fit."

"She left everything to the four of us," Maria's voice became hoarse. "I know it's been over a year, but I still can't believe Simone is gone."

"Neither can I," Cat cleared her throat. "But I thought we weren't going to start this day with tears."

"No, we're going to start this day with a smile and a good cup of coffee," Maria said, holding up her cup. "One thing my brother knows how to do is make coffee."

"Brett really does," Cat agreed with Maria, taking a sip of her coffee. "How is his wife, Alice, doing after she fell off her horse?"

"Alice has a few bruised ribs, and she broke her ankle," Maria told Cat. "She won't be riding for a while, and she has to keep off her feet for a few days."

"Oh no," Cat said. "I tried to wait up for you all to come back from the hospital, but I'm still not used to the country air."

"I've been back for ten months and I'm still not fully acclimatized." Maria looked out at the mountains. "I wish that my system bounced back as quickly as our sons' did."

"To be in our late twenties again like Liam and Indy." Maria sighed.

"I know, when I see Liam just bounce back..." Cat shook her head. "How is Indy's horse?"

"Pirate is going to be fine," Maria assured Cat. "He got a stone under his shoe and the vet managed to get it before it caused problems."

"I'm glad. I know Indy loves that horse," Cat said, sipping her coffee. "It's the last present Simone gave him."

"He is a beautiful horse," Maria told Cat. "I think Indy is right to want to eventually breed him when the time is right."

"Typical Indy planning so far ahead into the future," Cat laughed. "Pirate is still a young horse."

"I've already had quite a few of the ranchers asking about Pirate." Maria put her coffee cup down on the table. "You can tell the horse is from King Callum's bloodline."

"My father was lucky; King was the most beautiful horse and so are all his offspring." Cat finished her coffee. "Magenta, my horse from King's line, will be here later today."

"I'll take care of her," Maria promised. "I know how jittery she is after traveling."

"You really should've become a vet," Cat told her. "Specializing in horses. You're like a horse whisperer."

"Thank you, but working with horses is more of a calling and what I do is for pleasure." Maria smiled. "Magenta also knows me so there'll be no biting, stomping, or kicking."

"She can be a bit high-strung." Cat sighed. "I think that's because you've spoiled her."

"Sure, blame me." Maria laughed. "I know her sister, Sprite, will be happy to see her. Sprite has been missing Magenta and she didn't travel well to Montana."

"I believe poor Sprite was unwell when she was transported here," Cat said.

"She got a bit of travel sickness," Maria explained. "Luckily it was mild and was caught in time."

"Is she okay now?" Cat asked, concern shadowing her eyes.

"Yes, this morning I took her for her third long ride since she arrived at the ranch," Maria told her. "Sprite loves the letting loose on the open plains, so I had to keep reining her in."

"I can't wait to ride Magenta out in the fields," Cat admitted. "I was going to ask if I could ride one of your horses and if you'd come with me for a ride to Cupid's Bow."

"Are you sure you're ready to go back there?" Maria asked. It was her turn to be concerned. "When did you speak to Zac last?"

"About two years ago when I invested in the stable expansion for Cupid's Bow Ranch," Cat told her. "It was just after that, that Marshall and I eloped. Then my life took off on an exhausting emotional roller-coaster ride of treachery and deceit."

"If I had still been in Nashville, I would've stopped you from running off with that Marshall Myers lout." Maria's voice was laced with anger and disgust. "I'm so sorry I wasn't there for you."

"Maria, this isn't your fault," Cat assured her. "This was all me trying to mend a broken heart with an infatuation."

"I blame your lying, cheating, first husband," Maria said, defending Cat's honor. "He took advantage of your trust in him."

"You are the best friend anyone could ever wish for." Cat laughed. "Since the day we took off for Nashville together I've never once felt like I was alone in the world. You were always there pushing me up that mountain to achieve my goals. Never letting me slide when I thought I was tumbling down, and helping me heal when my heart got broken."

"Gosh, Cat, you did all that for me too," Maria reminded her. "I don't know where I would've been if you and Ashley hadn't stumbled upon me hiking to Billings thirty-one years ago."

"I actually can't believe it was so long ago," Cat said.

"I know, I feel so old." Maria laughed. "Now we have adult sons, nephews, and nieces."

"Speaking of our adult sons, isn't that Liam and Indy riding into the ranch?" Cat pointed to two riders speeding in through the backway of Big Valley Ranch.

"Yes, it is." Maria frowned, standing up and walking to the rail of the balcony. "Hey, you two," she called down to Indy and Liam as they rode right up to the back of the ranch house. "Is everything okay? You came in riding hot there."

"Hi Aunt Maria, is my mom here?" Indy called up to her.

"Hi, mom," Liam said.

"Hi, boys," Maria answered. "Yes, your mom's here."

"Hi, Indy," Cat said, looking over the balcony. "Is something wrong?"

"It's Uncle Zac, he's fallen down by the creek and won't let us call an ambulance," Indy told her. "I thought I'd come get you and Uncle Brett."

"Uncle Brett?" Cat frowned and looked at Maria. "I didn't think Brett and Zac were on speaking terms."

"All five ranchers have called a mutual ceasefire to the feud since the trouble on the ranches began," Maria told her. "How badly is Zac hurt?" She looked down at Indy and Liam.

"His ankle is badly sprained, and I think he may have two cracked ribs," Liam, who was doing a medical internship at the

Lewistown Hospital told her. "Can I get your medical kit, mom? I think I can make Uncle Zac comfortable enough to get him to the hospital."

"Good luck with that," Maria told him. "Zac hates hospitals."

"We'll be with you in a few minutes," Cat told Liam and Indy. "Can you get one of the horses ready for me, please Liam?"

"Ask one of the stable hands to get Lone Star ready for Cat," Maria told Liam.

"Sure," Liam nodded, sliding off his horse and walking it off towards the stables.

"I'll go find Uncle Brett," Indy told them.

"Cat, I'll meet you downstairs," Maria said, walking towards the bedroom door. "I'll go get the medical kit for Liam."

Cat nodded, heading for the bathroom where she quickly brushed her teeth and pulled her shoulder-length dark brown hair into a ponytail. She went back into the room to put on some jeans, a red light flannel, a shirt, her boots, and her black Stetson. Cat slid her phone into the front pocket of her jeans before going down to the kitchen to find Maria.

Chapter Two

THE ZAC AND CHELSEA SAGA - PART ONE

"This place has changed so much," Cat said as they rode their horses towards Bow Creek where Zac had his accident.

"Uncle Zac has been fixing up hiking trails for the Country Inn," Indy told Cat.

"The what?" Cat frowned.

"The Cupids Bow Country Inn," Indy repeated.

"I don't understand," Cat said stupidly, a frown creasing her brow. "Cupid's Bow Ranch is now a Country Inn?"

"Cat, can we talk about this later?" Maria glared at Indy. "We need to get to Zac."

"Yes." Cat's eyes narrowed. "Let's get to Zac." Her voice roughened with anger.

By the time they got to the area where Zac had had his accident Cat had worked up a head of steam.

How dare Zac turn Cupid's Bow Ranch into a country inn without her approval? Was the thought that her reeling mind kept landing on.

"Uncle Zac," Indy shouted when they came to the spot where Indy and Liam had left him. "Liam, he's passed out."

Indy and Liam slid off the back of their horses. Liam grabbed the medical kit and rushed over to Zac's side. Cat,

Brett, and Maria also dismounted to follow the young men. Cat's heart froze and the anger bubbling inside vanished when she saw her brother lying on the rocks. He looked pale and lifeless.

"Zac!" Cat shouted, starting to rush forward only to have a strong pair of arms stop her.

"Let Liam work," a deep, familiar voice said softly into her ear as he held her tightly against him.

"Let me go!" Cat hissed. "I need to go to my brother."

"Cat, David is right," Maria's face was just as pale as Cat imagined hers must be. "Brett has gone to lend a hand."

"I'm going to let you go now," David Miller, the Cupid's Bow Ranch foreman, and Zac's good friend told Cat. "I'm sure Zac is going to be okay. He passed out from the pain. I checked his pulse and made him as comfortable as I could."

"You've been here with him the whole time?" Cat didn't trust herself to turn and look into David's eyes.

The minute his arms had closed around her waist her heart had gone from frozen to one-hundred miles an hour. Instead, she stood watching as Liam did what he could before the medical chopper arrived. Conflicting emotions zinged through Cat. She felt guilty for getting angry with Zac when she'd found out about the inn. Then when she'd seen him lying there, images of finding their father lying still flashed through her mind. Fear had gripped her and stopped her from breathing for a few seconds before the adrenaline had kicked in and spurred her on toward Zac.

The chopper arrived and David went to secure all the horses. The minute he left her side, Cat felt oddly alone, cold, and terrified. She'd had to stop herself from reaching out to David and stopping him from going. Instead, she linked her hand with Maria's for support while they stood watching the medics load Zac onto the chopper.

"I'll go with Uncle Zac," Liam told Cat, giving her upper arm a comforting squeeze. "Uncle Brett said he'd bring you and mom to the hospital."

"I'm going to get Hayden and Jamie," Indy said. "They need to know their father has had an accident."

"You didn't call them right away?" Cat frowned.

"I don't have my phone with me," Indy explained. "I forgot it back at the ranch."

"Do you want me to call them?" Cat's hand shook as pulled her phone out of her pocket.

"No, mom," Indy gave her a small smile. "It's best if I go see them face to face. They're both back at the ranch."

"Okay," Cat agreed. "I'm going to go back to Big Valley Ranch with Maria and Brett. We'll meet you at the hospital."

"Mom," Indy pulled Cat to him for a hug, "Uncle Zac is going to be okay."

"I'm sure he is," Cat said, her voice growing hoarse as she bit back the tears.

"I'll see you at the hospital," Indy promised, going over to where David was keeping the horses calm.

"What happened to Zac?" Cat asked, watching the chopper take off.

"We were mapping out a hiking trail that would lead to picnic spots here by Bow Creek when we found some dead deer at the water's edge." David walked up behind them, leading the horses. "Zac and I came back with the pickup to get the animals. But they were gone and that's when we found fresh tracks leading back to Four Lakes Ranch."

Cat was forced to turn around and look into his hazel eyes. Eyes that she could still remember so well from almost thirty-two years ago, the day she and David had first met.

"Why would the Becketts, who own Four Lakes, take dead deer?" Maria asked David while all Cat could do was force herself to look away from David's captivating stare and look towards the creek.

"They didn't," David told her. "But we think Ron Hicks or some of his ranch hands did."

"Hicks?" Cat managed to find her voice.

"Yes, Ron Hicks took over the Donaldson ranch that borders Four Lakes Ranch," Maria explained to Cat.

"What happened to old man Donaldson who owned the Donaldson Ranch?" Cat's eyes widened.

"He passed away quite a few years ago," Brett told her. "We thought Ron Hicks had bought the farm, but it turned out that he was old man Donaldson's grandson."

"I didn't even know he had children," Cat said.

Maria surprised Cat by saying, "He had a son and three daughters, apparently. His son and eldest daughter died in some car accident long before any of us were born."

"His wife left him after that, taking their other two daughters with her," Brett carried on the story for Cat. "When he died, Ron and some cousin we've never seen or heard of inherited the Donaldson Ranch."

"I'll catch you up on the Hicks story later," Maria promised Cat.

"What had happened to the deer?" Brett asked David while they mounted their horses.

"That's what we were hoping to find out. We wanted to take the animals to the vet clinic." David swung up onto his horse and they started back towards their ranches. "When we looked them over there were no bite marks or bullet wounds on the animals."

"Are you thinking they may have been poisoned?" Brett's eyes widened and he glanced back at the river. "We all pull water that comes from this river for our animals and crops, and it feeds the wells that come into our houses."

"I've managed to take some water samples," David assured Brett. "That's what we were doing when two hooded men attacked us. Liam has them with him."

"Indy said Zac fell," Cat's voice echoed her alarm at hearing they were attacked.

"You said you came back to get the animals, not to take water samples," Maria said, looking confused.

"If you'd all let me finish what I was trying to tell you instead of veering off into a million different side conversations…" David pointed out.

"Sorry," Brett butted in before either Maria or Cat could say another word. "Continue from where you were telling us about tracing the tracks back to Four Lakes Ranch."

"Thank you." David tipped his hat. "A few days ago, some of the cattle became ill. We lost a few of them while others are still at the vet. They'd been poisoned."

"Do you think they drank from the river?" Cat asked.

"We're still not sure," David said. "We called Indy to bring us some jars so we could collect water samples. A few minutes before Indy and Liam arrived the two thugs appeared."

"Do you think they were looking for more dead animals?" Maria asked.

"I'm not sure," David told her. "But they came right for us. Almost as if we were their targets." He shook his head. "We fought them off but as soon as they saw Indy and Liam, they turned to leave but Zac wasn't letting them go. He ran after them. I tried to stop Zac but before I could the two men ganged up on him. One hit him in the ribs and the other pushed him. He lost his footing and fell onto the rocks."

"Oh, my word!" Cat breathed. "Why would they try to attack you and Zac?"

"I can't answer that either," David told her. "But trust me when I tell you, I'm going to find out."

"A lot of strange things have been happening around us over these last couple of years," Brett said.

"Why didn't Zac or Indy tell me about this?" Cat looked at Maria questioningly. "Why didn't you say anything to me?"

"I've only started hearing about any of this in the past month." Maria looked at Cat. "I haven't had the chance to catch you up on what I know as you've only been back for two days."

"Sorry," Cat said. "I didn't mean to sound so harsh. I just can't believe my brother got attacked on our own land." She shook her head. "I used to feel so safe here on the ranch."

"I know," Maria nodded. "Let's get to the hospital and I'll tell you what I know along the way."

"How is he?" Cat asked Indy as she, Maria, and Brett walked into the hospital where Zac was.

"The doctor is going to come let us know as soon as he has any news," Indy told her. "Jamie and Hayden are here. They're in the family waiting area near Zac's room."

"I'll go get us all some coffee," Brett offered. "Would you help me please, Indy?"

"Of course, Uncle Brett," Indy said, looking at Cat. "We'll meet you there. Go straight down that hall and it's the first family room on the right."

"We'll see you there." Brett turned and walked off towards the cafeteria with Indy.

"I feel so terrible." Cat's eyes misted over. "This is my third day back in Lewistown and I haven't been to see Zac." She looked down. "I should've called him, but all I did was send him a text to tell him I'm here."

"Cat, you've been going through a lot," Maria reminded her. "You needed to climb into your shell for a few days and get your head straight. Zac understands that."

"I don't think he does," Cat said, looking up at Maria. "He didn't message back until late last night and all he said was that we need to talk."

"I know that he's missed you," Maria told her. "Zac's been over to the ranch numerous times these past two months because of what has been happening on the ranches."

"You still haven't told me what's been going on." Cat and Maria started walking down the long sterile passageway.

"Cat?" A familiar female voice came from behind them that made Cat freeze.

Cat and Maria turned to find Chelsea Hitchin, Zac's ex-wife and mother of his children. She was also one of Cat's ex-best friends. Their friendship had ended on a bad note when Cat found out that she was in a secret relationship with Zac. Cat could overlook the fact that Chelsea had broken their sacred friendship pact. A pact they had made when she, Chelsea, and Ashley had turned thirteen.

The three of them had vowed not to date each other's brothers or cousins. It had been a silly, young pact because you can't choose who you fall in love with. But you can choose not to lie to your friends. Cat had even forgiven Chelsea for lying to her and Ashley about the time she'd blown them off to secretly meet Zac. But there were some lies and actions that Cat would still never be able to forget, even if she could somehow find it in her heart to forgive her and trust her again.

Cat stood staring at Chelsea, not quite knowing what to say and not trusting herself to say anything because she knew she had nothing nice to say to her.

"Hi, Chelsea," Maria said, breaking the tension that had sprung up between Cat and Chelsea.

"Hello, Maria," Chelsea greeted her, her eyes sliding away from Cat's. A sad shadow flitted through them. "Has the doctor said anything about how Zac is?"

"Why would you care?" Cat asked, not able to stop herself as the angry words slipped off her tongue. "The two of you have been divorced for over twelve years now."

"Cat!" Maria turned and looked at her, shocked.

"Well, it's true," Cat shrugged. Once the words had broken passed her lips, she found she was unable to stop the rest that tumbled out. "I thought you'd moved on and out of Zac's life with the ex-foreman, Harris Conway, and broke up his marriage as well."

"Cat!" Ashley hissed, walking in behind Chelsea and overhearing what she'd just said.

"Ashley?" Cat frowned, seeing her best friend. "Why are you here?"

"Chelsea's car is in the shop, so she asked me for a lift,"

Ashley explained. "I brought Chelsea to the hospital when she heard about Zac."

"Thank you for coming," Cat gave Ashley a tight smile. "But they're only letting the family see him when the doctor says we can go through. Jamie and Hayden along with Liam are in the family area near Zac's room"

"Chelsea is family," Ashley pointed out.

"No, she's not," Cat disagreed. Her voice dripped with ice as she glanced at Chelsea. "The moment Chelsea filed for divorce and got engaged to another man she severed all ties with the Sparrow family." She looked back at Ashley. "As the Sparrow family's appointed lawyer, you should know that."

"Cat!" Ashley's eyes narrowed and she shook her head. "Your brother is lying in intensive care. Now is not the time for this."

"You're right," Cat said and once again looked at Chelsea. "You and Chelsea can wait out here. I'll send someone to let you both know how my brother is when we have news."

Cat gave Chelsea one last cold glare before spinning on her heel and marching off.

"I'm sorry," Maria apologized. "I'll come and let you know when there is news," Cat heard Maria say as she continued to march down the passage.

"Hi, Aunty Cat," Jamie, Zac's youngest child, greeted her. Jamie was now a full-grown woman with a family of her own.

"Hi, honey." Cat hugged her. "Any word on your father?" She greeted Zac's oldest, Hayden.

"Hi, Aunty Cat." Hayden kissed her cheek. "No, we're still waiting. Liam did pop in a few minutes ago to tell us that they were just waiting on some test results."

"Test results?" Cat frowned.

"Yes, they took some blood," Hayden explained. "Liam was

worried that my dad may have consumed some of the water from the river when he fell."

"When dad fell, he hit the rocks and landed in some of the river water," Jamie took over from Hayden. "He also cut himself on the rocks and they need to check for any infectious bacteria."

"Good," Cat nodded. "Did Liam say anything about the water tests?"

"No." Hayden shook his head. "He said that they would only have those tests back in a couple of hours, even with the rush he put on them."

"In the meantime, we've got Janine buying up a year's worth of bottled water," Jamie told Cat.

"Who is Janine?" Cat's brows furrowed.

"Janine Tanner, Bessie's niece," Hayden told Cat. "She's the Cupid's Bow Inn Manager."

"Janine Tanner is working for us now?" Cat's eyes narrowed.

She knew Janine because Bessie had been her family's housekeeper since before Cat had been born. Janine had often visited Bessie when they were growing up and had loved Cupid's Bow Ranch. Cat had even taught her how to ride a horse and rope a steer. Cat decided she wasn't going to quiz Zac's children about how her home had become a country inn. That was between her and Zac.

When Zac had sufficiently recovered, they were going to have a serious conversation about his going behind her back. Cat had never agreed to the ranch becoming Cupid's Bow Inn. She couldn't believe that her entire family, including her son, had kept quiet about it for all these years. But like Ashley had pointed out, this was not the time for Cat's grievances. Zac was hurt and there would be plenty of time when he was better to have it out with him.

"Cat, can I have a word?" Maria asked her, pulling her to one side. Cat nodded.

"What's wrong?" Cat asked.

"You were quite harsh to Chelsea," Maria told her. "I think

you should let her be here with her kids. She and Zac were married for a long time."

"They've also been divorced for a long time, and trust me on this," Cat said, "Zac wouldn't want her here."

"Zac and Chelsea have a good, co-parent relationship," Maria argued. "I think he would want her here."

"No," Jamie interrupted, "Aunt Cat is right, Aunt Maria." She pulled a face. "Sorry for eavesdropping."

"You're never sorry for eavesdropping, little sister." Hayden shook his head. "But they are both right, Aunt Maria. Dad wouldn't want mom here."

"Okay," Maria said, holding up her hands. "But your mother is out there looking deathly pale with worry for Zac."

"I'll go speak to her," Hayden volunteered.

"Thanks, big brother." Jamie gave him a grateful smile as he left the room.

"Okay, I'm beginning to think I've missed something here," Maria's eyes narrowed as she looked from Jamie to Cat.

"My parents are in the middle of a custody battle," Jamie told Maria, whose frown deepened even more upon hearing that.

"Do they have another child I don't know about?" Maria asked.

"No," Cat shook her head. "It's over horses."

Chapter Three

THE ZAC AND CHELSEA SAGA - PART TWO

"Horses?" Maria raised her eyebrows looking amazed. "Are these special horses?"

"Yes," Cat and Jamie said together.

"It's a long story." Cat shook her head. "It's amazing how petty people can get when a relationship ends."

"We're not going anywhere for a while," Maria pointed out, before taking a seat and looking up at Cat and Jamie, waiting to hear the story. "I would love to hear about yet another feud the Sparrow family is involved in."

Cat took the chair facing Maria while Jamie sat next to Cat.

"My parents started fostering retired and mistreated horses while my father was studying to become a vet," Jamie explained to Maria.

"Yes, I remember that." Maria nodded. "Cat told me that's why your father needed to build more stables and create more corrals."

"When my mom moved out, my father carried on fostering horses," Jamie told them. "A few months before their divorce was finalized, my father got word about a badly mistreated horse."

"Zac needed Chelsea's help to get the horse," Jamie continued the story. "When they got to the place where the horse was being kept my parents were horrified at the state of the horse."

"My father also recognized the horse to be an Arabian," Jamie told Maria. "The horse's owner didn't even have a name for her. My father said the horse was so thin and shied away from people."

"The owner had bought the mare to breed as she came from good stock. That was all the man would tell Zac." Cat's eyes flashed with anger. She couldn't stand people who mistreated animals. "But the mare wouldn't take a stud; she'd go wild, and the owner had to pay out for damages to the studs that were brought to him."

"I take it the studs were also Arabian's so I can imagine why the man wasn't happy," Maria said before her eyes too flashed with anger. "But that's no excuse to mistreat a horse."

"Apparently they were Arabian's being bred for racing," Cat confirmed Maria's suspicions about the breed of the stud horses.

"The man was also not happy to let the animal go, but my father threatened to close down his entire operation if he didn't let them take the mare." Jamie's phone bleeped and she pulled it out of her pocket before continuing. "Sorry, this is my au pair, she's taken my daughters to the park. I have to take it." Jamie got up and walked out of the room.

"Getting back to the story," Cat picked up where Jamie left off, "Zac spent hours getting the mare back in shape and winning over her trust. He named her Mystique."

"I remember you mentioning Zac had a new Arabian called Mystique." Maria nodded. "I still wondered why he needed an Arabian. I thought you bred quarter horses."

"That's right." Cat laughed. "Mystique was a beautiful horse."

"You sent me pictures of her," Maria reminded Cat. "She was pitch black with one white sock."

"Yes, that's right." Cat nodded. "It was that sock that helped Zac identify who she really was. To his amazement, he found out that Mystique was actually Seasprite."

"The Seasprite?" Maria's brows creased. "The legendary

endurance racer? The one that was supposed to have died when her horsebox overturned when being transported home?"

"Yes," Cat nodded. "If you remember, Seasprite had become lame during her last endurance race after taking a tumble."

"Seasprite's owners were concerned about her not being able to race again," Maria remembered. "Two days after her owners mentioned this, there was an accident that involved the pickup transporting her back to her then owner's ranch."

"I guess having to keep her even to breed would've cost too much." Cat shook her head in disgust.

"So instead, they faked her death and sold her to a stud farm," Maria guessed.

"They also claimed the insurance money for Seasprite," Jamie told them, re-entering the room.

"Good old insurance fraud," Maria shuddered. "How cold and callous can people get? Seasprite was used to only the best of everything right up until she had a bad fall. Then she gets tossed aside like yesterday's garbage once she can't perform anymore."

"Well, that family got their just deserts," Jamie assured Maria. "They lost their entire stables."

"I'm not a vindictive person but I'm glad they're not in operation anymore," Maria said. "Horses aren't a novelty. Like dogs, cats, and other pets, they're a commitment as much as your human family are."

"Absolutely," Cat agreed.

"Now I know about how Zac came to have a purebred Arabian horse," Maria looked at Cat and Jamie. "Is Mystique the horse your parents are fighting over?"

"One of them," Jamie told Maria. "When my father got Mystique, my parents hadn't settled anything about their divorce. I'm not sure what the heck got into my mother, but she became a downright itchy-b."

"Jamie," Maria laughed. "That's no way to talk about your mother."

"There is no other way to describe her back then, Aunt

Maria," Jamie explained. "My mother was moody, sullen, and seemed to always be on edge."

"Maybe she was having second thoughts about leaving your father but realized there was no turning back from where she was," Maria offered an explanation. "I know when I first separated from my late husband, Jared, I was a bit like that too."

"A bit?" Cat said wide-eyed and harrumphed. "You were like a cat on a hot tin roof."

"Then maybe my mother should have at least tried couples therapy like my father suggested. Instead, she packed us up and dragged me away from Cupid Bow Ranch, our home!" Jamie's voice held traces of anger. "Hayden was lucky. He got to choose where he wanted to live. He also went away to university, so he never really got in the crossfire that followed my parents' separation."

"I'm sorry, sweetheart." Maria leaned forward and gave Jamie's hand a gentle squeeze. "It couldn't have been easy for you at only fourteen."

"I didn't even get to decide who I wanted to live with," Jamie said bitterly. "I had to divide my time between my mother and father." She shook her head. "But I preferred being with my father. My mother started seeing Harris Conway, Cupid's Bow former foreman."

"I believe he quit a week after Chelsea left Zac," Maria's eyes narrowed. "Were the rumors true about Chelsea and Harris?"

"I'm afraid so," Cat told Maria. "Not even two weeks after Chelsea and Zac's divorce came through Chelsea was talking about getting engaged to Harris."

"Ah," Maria nodded, "you never mentioned that part to me when you told me about Zac and Chelsea's breakup."

"I wasn't too sure if the rumor was true or not," Cat said. "You know how people talk in a small town, and then things get blown up like a bad photograph. All distorted and out of proportion."

"Wasn't Harris married?" Maria asked.

"Yes, he was," Cat confirmed. "I think he was going through a messy divorce himself at the same time Zac and Chelsea were."

"I never liked Harris," Jamie admitted.

"She really didn't," Cat backed up Jamie's statement. "When Jamie came to visit me in Nashville, she and Simone would talk in length about how much Jamie didn't trust Harris."

"I do remember Simone saying something about that to me," Maria told them. "I thought it was because he was seeing Chelsea and you blamed him for the divorce."

"Nope," Jamie shook her head. "I just never liked him."

"Zac never really warmed up to Harris either." Cat sat back in the uncomfortable chair. "Chelsea was the one who had insisted Zac hire him."

"Then not even four years later she runs off with the man?" Maria shook her head in disgust. "I'm beginning to see why you're so hostile towards Chelsea."

"My mother was an only child and I think she was a bit spoiled but my grandparents," Jamie tried to excuse her mother's actions.

"So how did Zac and Chelsea end up fighting for custody of the horses?" Maria moved the conversation back to the custody battle between Zac and Chelsea.

"My father bought another Arabian horse," Jamie continued the story. "Caesar."

"Was he another retired racehorse?" Maria asked.

"Yes, he was," Cat confirmed Maria's suspicions. "The difference between Caesar and Mystique was that Caesar's owner loved his horse. But the man was selling his ranch to go live in a retirement village, having no family of his own to leave the place to."

"My father got Caesar at an excellent price as his owner was just happy for his horse to go to a good place," Jamie explained. "I went with my father to fetch Caesar and, oh my word! You should've seen the stables at this place. My father has actually asked Indy to model the new stables around those."

"Did he have any other horses?" Maria looked at Jamie questioningly.

"No, he'd already sold them off over the years as he got older and was no longer able to keep up the ranch life pace," Jamie told Maria. "He hung onto Caesar until a few days before he left for the retirement village in Florida."

"Wow, that's quite a ways away from Montana." Cat laughed. "The man moved to the other side of the country."

"I guess most of the elderly think Florida is the ideal retirement place," Maria shrugged. "You can't beat the weather and there are a lot of other retirees there."

"That's great if you don't mind being bashed about by heavy storms," Cat said.

"Getting back to my story," Jamie said with raised eyebrows.

"Sorry, honey." Cat gave Jamie's arm a gentle squeeze.

"So was Zac wanting to breed Mystique?" Maria sat back in her chair, watching Jamie intently.

"Yes," Jamie nodded. "And he did manage to breed her with Caesar."

"Wow," Maria said, amazed. "Did they have a filly or colt?"

"A colt that I named Cupid," Jamie grinned.

"Your horse, Cupid?" Maria's eyes widened. "I've been meaning to come and see your horse."

"You'll love him," Jamie assured Maria. "He's quite the character."

"Zac helped Jamie train Cupid and they raced him, twice." Cat smiled proudly at Jamie. "My niece here is quite the horse trainer because Cupid won both of his endurance races."

"Cupid did so well that my father was getting amazing offers for him," Jamie told Maria. "But my father wouldn't sell him because he was my horse, and I wasn't going to sell him either."

"Instead, Zac bred Mystique and Caesar again," Cat explained. "Their second filly sold for an amazing price and the new owners asked Jamie to train the horse for them. They were so impressed with what Jamie had done with Cupid."

"I'm going to be breeding Cupid as well." Jamie smiled excitedly. "Dad has found an Arabian broodmare for him."

"And the custody battle?" Maria once again pulled the conversation back on track.

"Yes, we're getting to the ugly part." Jamie shook her head. "As you may know, things in the area haven't been too great for a while now. We had a bad few years for cattle and horses, so dad was planning to turn the ranch into an inn."

"How long has it been an inn for now?" Cat couldn't help asking.

"Since I was fifteen," Jamie told Cat. "He'd started working on it the year before that. But it was still small. A bed and breakfast really."

"Back on the topic," Maria snapped her fingers. "I'm dying to know about the custody battle."

"As you know, my gran is still very much alive and although my mother now runs the ranch, it isn't hers," Jamie got back on topic. "I know because I overheard the conversation that Harris lost everything in his divorce. He was trying to push my mom to put gran at an old age home."

"Was your mother gunning for a share of Cupids Bow Ranch?" Maria asked, shocked.

"Yes," Cat said, nodding. "She was."

"But not just the ranch," Jamie said. "She wanted a share of my father's horse breeding business."

"My brother's three new horses in particular," Cat told Maria.

"Three?" Maria's eyes narrowed. "Oh, you mean Cupid as well?"

"No, my mother wanted Monarch." Jamie shook her head and her eyes clouded over. "I couldn't believe my mother could become so grabby and mean."

"When people separate then go through a divorce there's a lot of mixed emotions boiling inside of them," Cat took Jamie's hand. "When children are involved, you want to try and keep things civil between you and your soon-to-be ex."

"It doesn't always work out that way though." Maria gave

Jamie a warm smile. "You think you have the flames of anger and hurt under control. But there are these tiny highly flammable embers floating about that ignite with the teeniest spark."

"Maria is right," Cat agreed with Maria's analogy. "I remember how hard it was for Indy when myself and Paul were getting a divorce."

"I know, I remember Indy telling me that Uncle Paul was barely out the front door when he had another woman on his arm," Jamie's voice had traces of bitterness in it. "I couldn't believe it when my mom started going on dates with Harris. It was only two weeks after we moved to Mountain Rise."

"Before we move completely off the topic again," Maria stopped Jamie's train of thought, "who is Monarch?"

"Oh, sorry, Aunt Maria," Jamie laughed. "Once two of Mystique and Caesar's offspring were showing signs of being incredible horses word got around about my father."

"And Jamie," Cat pointed out. "She may have only been a teen, but she has this incredible way with horses."

"I know," Maria smiled patiently at Cat.

"Another ex-breeder approached my father about a rare colt he had," Jamie told Maria. "I once again went with my dad to see the horse, and he was magnificent."

"I take it this was Monarch?" Maria asked.

"Yes, his coat shone with silky gold, and his eyes were the color of a fine whisky," Jamie smiled at the enthralled look on Maria's face. "He was an Akhal-Teke. The owner had got him when he was a few days old. The breeder was selling him at a reduced rate because they thought he was deformed."

"Why?" Maria looked at Jamie wide-eyed.

"He was small, he couldn't walk well, he kept falling over, and they didn't think he was going to live too long," Jamie answered the question. "Little did they know the horse was going to grow to well over the average sixteen-hands for that breed."

"I haven't seen Monarch in the flesh, but the pictures Zac and Jamie have sent me over the years he is incredibly beautiful,"

Cat told Maria. "The classic case of a runt growing up to be the most beautiful and strongest."

"I really need to go look at Zac's new stables." Maria sighed. "So, Zac now has two Arabians and an Akhal-Teke?"

"He does." Jamie nodded and laughed. "And it's four Arabians now if you include Cupid and his sister Tara."

"When Zac got Monarch, his divorce still wasn't final." Cat shook her head. "My brother was stalling, not Chelsea, who was chomping at the bit to have the divorce finalized."

"Aunt Cat is not exaggerating about that either," Jamie said. "It took nearly three years for their divorce to be finalized, and my mother was pushing to get it over."

"Did Chelsea get any of the horses?" Maria asked.

"No. My father's lawyer made it quite clear that the prenup they'd signed was ironclad," Jamie answered Maria. "If anything happened to my father while they were still married, my mother would always have a place to stay. But she'd never own any part of Cupid's Bow Ranch."

"If Chelsea did leave, she'd do so with nothing more than her clothes and whatever she'd bought during the marriage," Cat explained. "It was the same prenup both my husbands had to sign."

"Wow, your father really was protecting this land," Maria said to Cat.

"Yes, just like your parents would've protected Big Valley Ranch." Cat nodded. "Did you ever read the prenup that Jared had to sign when you two got married?" she asked Maria.

"No," Maria frowned, "I didn't even know there was a prenup."

"We all had to get our spouses to sign one before getting married," Jamie told Maria. "All the four ranches that border Cupids Bow have to remain in the direct family line."

"What?" Maria looked confused. "Why?"

"It has something to do with the land lease agreement signed by the five original landowners of the five ranches hundreds of years ago." Jamie bit her lip thoughtfully. "I've been meaning to find out about that actually."

"To wrap up your story about the custody battle," Maria went on, "is your mother still trying to get half of your father's horse breeding business?"

"The battle went on between my mother and father for years." Jamie shook her head. "My father had to stop breeding all the horses, including the quarter horses, until the issue was resolved."

"That's why the ranch started to get into debt?" Cat looked at Jamie, realization suddenly dawning on her. "Zac turned Cupid's Bow into an inn to save our land because of Chelsea?"

Anger spurted through Cat. Chelsea couldn't steal Cupid's Bow away from the Sparrow's, so she tried to destroy it instead.

"Aunt Cat, I don't think it was my mother," Jamie defended Chelsea. "We're pretty sure Harris was the one influencing mom to get her share of Cupid's Bow. Which meant that if she was entitled to half of the ranch, dad would have to buy her out."

"But when she realized there was an ironclad prenup about the property, she tried to take away the ranch's biggest source of income," Maria guessed. "So, she never really wanted the horses, after all, she was trying to bankrupt the ranch?"

"No, I don't think that was her intention," Jamie stood up for her mother. "She'd given up her nursing career to stay home with myself and Hayden. My mother had also helped my father start his vet practice. I guess she thought she deserved a little more than her suitcase full of clothes."

"Is she still trying to get your father's horses?" Maria looked at Jamie.

"No. After years of tug of war and her nearly bankrupting my father because he couldn't keep the breeding program going, she suddenly backed off one day," Jamie told her.

"Yes, right after Harris left her and ran away with the young waitress he'd been seeing on the side," Cat said with malice in her voice.

"Do you think it was Harris that was influencing Chelsea to get half of Zac's business?" Maria asked Cat but Jamie answered.

"My gran and I do," Jamie said honestly. "My gran kept telling my mother that she hardly recognized her since she started dating Harris."

"Even Hayden said how much his mother had changed," Cat told Maria. "And you know how much Hayden loves and protects his mother."

"I don't get it," Maria shook her head. "Chelsea doesn't strike me as the type to be influenced like that." Her brow furrowed. "Maybe something else was going on."

"That's what we all thought as well," Jamie shook her head. "To this day Hayden still thinks that Harris was somehow manipulating our mother. Harris never really liked our father."

"Did your mother know Harris before he came to work at Cupids Bow?" Maria looked curiously at Jamie.

"I don't think so," Jamie frowned. "I've never asked her." She looked questioningly at Cat.

Before Jamie could ask Cat about it the door opened, and Liam and another doctor stepped into the room, saving Cat from an awkward situation. As she turned away, Cat noticed Maria looking at her thoughtfully as if she knew that Cat was hiding something.

Chapter Four

RETURN TO CUPIDS BOW RANCH - PART TWO

Cat stood staring at her childhood home. Zac had kept the main house almost the same as it always was on the outside. All that was different was the sign above the roof that covered the front porch, Cupids Bow Country Inn. Cat teetered between anger and sadness that her home was now open to complete strangers. Jamie had told her that Zac had left her room untouched for when she came home, which was sweet of him, considering he probably needed it for guests. It still didn't make up for the fact that he'd turned Cupids Bow Ranch house into a country inn without her knowledge.

Cat wasn't sure if she'd be staying at the ranch, but she was there for when they brought Zac home. He had a few fractured ribs, a sprained ankle, and stitches in his head. The doctor said that Zac needed to keep off his feet for at least a week. Cat had agreed to stop by to help him out during the day because his daughter, Jamie, and son, Hayden, worked during the day. At night they could help him as they both lived on the ranch already. Zac had built five extra houses on the ranch. One for himself, one for Hayden, one for Jamie, one for her, and one for Indy.

Cat hadn't had the conversation with Zac about him turning the ranch into an inn without her consent yet. She wanted to wait until he was back home, out of the hospital. Right now, she had to step through the front door and get the keys to Zac's house. Cat took a deep breath, pushed down the door handle, and stepped inside. She swallowed as she looked around at what was now the foyer. Zac had done it quite tastefully as he'd tried to keep the essence of the original ranch house. Cat's heart felt heavy as she pictured her home filled with people she didn't know. But she shook the feeling off and walked up to the front desk where a young woman was working on a computer.

"Hello, welcome to Cupids Bow Country Inn." The woman smiled cheerfully when she saw Cat. "Do you have a reservation with us?"

As soon as the woman recognized Cat, her eyes widened. Cat had seen that look on fans' faces many times, but at least this woman had the decorum not to fawn over her or melt at the sight of her. Instead, she continued to smile sweetly and treat Cat with the respect she obviously offered all her guests.

"No," Cat said a little abruptly.

Cat didn't mean for it to come out that way. But she wasn't used to being asked if she had a reservation for her own home. It had immediately sparked the anger boiling inside of her over her home being turned into a tourist attraction.

"Oh no, that's unfortunate because we're fully booked, I'm afraid." The young woman looked genuinely sorry. "You know, my boss does keep one room vacant for his sister. But in all the years I have worked here I've never seen her. Let me call the manager and see if she can maybe give you that room."

Cat knew the woman was trying her best to accommodate her and didn't have the heart to tell her that the room Zac had reserved was for her. The woman had not yet seemed to put together the fact that her name was Cat Sparrow and she shared Zac's last name.

"That won't be necessary," a female voice came from behind a speechless Cat who was standing and staring at the woman in amazement.

"Ah, here's my manager now," the young woman said pointing

behind Cat who slowly turned around to see Janine Tanner, their old housekeeper's niece.

"This is Zac's elusive sister." Janine smiled at the woman before stepping up to greet Cat with a hug. "You haven't changed a bit."

"Hello, Janine." Cat smiled. "Neither have you," she returned the compliment.

"Jamie did tell me you were back in Montana and staying with the Parkers over at Big Valley Ranch." Janine turned and looked at the woman behind the desk. "Sally, meet Cat Sparrow. Cat, this is Sally, our front desk administrator."

"Cat Sparrow?" Sally's eyes widened. "*The* Cat Sparrow is Zac's sister?"

"Uh..." Cat looked at Janine for help.

"Yes," Janine stepped in. "And as with all the famous guests we've had through here, we expect discretion from you to protect Cat's privacy while she's in Montana."

"Of course," Sally agreed. "I'm sorry, but it's such a pleasure to meet you. I'm a huge fan of your music."

"Thank you," Cat said.

"And for the record," Sally told Cat, "I don't believe a word that lying Marshall Myers said about you."

"That's very kind of you." Cat gave her a small smile, starting to feel a little uncomfortable with the way the conversation was going.

"It's so obvious that you were the one who wrote his last three hit songs, just like his other ex-girlfriend did before you," Sally stated.

"Excuse me?" Cat frowned at what Sally had just said. "What do you mean?"

"You didn't know?" Sally looked at Cat surprised.

"Sally," Janine admonished the young woman, "you know better than to gossip."

"I'm sorry," Sally apologized. "Janine is right; I'm stepping out of line and disrespecting the privacy of our guests."

"Cat's here for Zac's spare keys to his house," Janine quickly changed the conversation. "Could you please get them for her, and I'll show her to the house."

"Of course." Sally nodded and walked through to the back room leading off the reception. She returned a few minutes later. "Here you go. I've also included a booklet with some of the activities we now offer at the ranch for our guests."

"I'm sure Cat's not interested in those," Janine said.

"No, I'd like to see what the ranch offers," Cat thanked Sally and took the information guide booklet along with the key.

"It was so nice to meet you," Sally said with a big smile on her face. "If you need anything I'm at the desk from seven in the morning until six in the evening."

"Thank you, Sally." Cat turned and followed Janine through the house.

"It must be such a shock seeing all the changes Zac has made." Janine guided Cat through the back living room. The room led onto the large dining area and through to the kitchen.

"Zac turned the family room and dining area into an open-plan space." Cat looked around the room before walking into the kitchen where she stopped. "He didn't change the kitchen that much."

"The only difference is the large walk-in pantry," Janine showed Cat. "Zac broke through to the laundry room."

"Oh, wow!" Cat stepped into the large room. "It's huge, and so well organized." Her eyes caught the large fridge at the end of the room. "Is that a cold storage area?"

"Yes," Janine confirmed.

"Where's the laundry?" Cat asked.

"One of the outbuildings that was used as a storage shed is now the laundry," Janine told her. "Would you like to see it?" She grinned proudly. "It is quite impressive."

"Sure, I have some time before Zac gets home," Cat said.

Janine led the way through the back door and out into the back garden. They crossed the lawn to the shed that she once played in, which had been expanded into a large laundry room.

There were four washers and dryers, a few ironing stations, trouser presses, and folding stations.

"Very nice." Cat nodded, impressed.

"We save a lot of money doing all our own laundry for both the inn and ranch." Janine walked out of the building. "Zac's house is this way."

Janine led Cat around the back of the laundry. They followed a neatly done stone walkway down a slight hill to where the ranch hand housing used to be. Where there once were twelve small housing units now stood six double-story houses. Each one had their own fenced-off front garden. Zac had designed them to look like a small neighborhood. Three houses stood side by side facing the other three houses. The back garden walls were a lot higher so passersby couldn't see into them.

"The ranch hand cottages look a lot different," Cat said. "Zac has put a lot of work into the ranch over the past thirty-one years."

"He has," Janine agreed. "House number six is rented out as a self-catering house."

"Do guests actually want such a big house for a vacation home?" Cat asked.

"Yes," Janine told her. "This house is quite popular. So much so that Zac has been toying with the idea of making a few more self-catering bungalows."

"Is the inn popular?" Cat walked through the gate of house number three.

"It is." Janine walked Cat to the front door. "This is Zac's house."

"Thank you," Cat said.

"Cat, I know you didn't approve of turning Cupids Bow Ranch into a country inn." Janine looked at her. "But you must know it was the only way of keeping the place going after everything that's happened."

"What do you mean, everything that's happened?" Cat's eyes narrowed.

"I think it's best that Zac explains that to you." Janine gave her a small smile. "I'd better get back to work. We have a wedding party arriving this afternoon."

"We do weddings now as well?" Cat looked at Janine in surprise.

"Yes, country weddings have become quite the thing," Janine explained. "We offer a whole week of activities for the bride and groom parties to partake in."

"Nice." Cat nodded.

Janine said her goodbyes and left Cat standing alone on Zac's front porch looking around the little neighborhood he'd made in what used to be their back garden. She sighed before turning to open the front door. Cat was surprised to see that Zac had furnished his house with the furniture from the ranch house. She'd wondered where all their antique furniture had gone. The Sparrow ranch house had been full of furniture from generations of Sparrows that had lived in it.

Cat walked through the bright and airy house to the kitchen where she threw her purse, keys, and the venue booklet Sally, the young woman at the front desk, had given her. The booklet skidded off the counter and landed on the floor. When Cat bent down to pick it up a note fell out of it.

I have a lot more information for you. Contact me.

There was a mobile number and no name on the note. Cat stared at the note thoughtfully, thinking that it must've been Sally who put it in there. She would give her a call when she had a free moment. Cat was curious about the statement Sally had made. She knew it was probably just rumors and trash magazine gossip Sally had to tell her. But at this point in Cat's messed up life, she'd grasp at any straw there was to get out of this quicksand puddle of trouble she was in. Cat put the note back into the booklet and left it next to her purse on the kitchen counter. She went through to the spare room on the ground floor and started to get it ready for Zac. While she worked, her mind drifted back over the past year. It had been three years after her divorce when

Cat had met country singer Marshal Myers. She'd got swept up by his boyish good looks and silky smooth charm. Cat had heard all the rumors about Marshall being a leech who attached himself to the latest top country singing star. He then used them to promote his own career by convincing them to help him write his latest song.

Even West had tried to warn Cat not to do a song with him. A song which she had to write, and her record company produced. The song had gone straight to number one mainly because of her name on it. Cat's fans were also enthralled by their budding romance. Of course, Cat's PR company had jumped on that and splashed their love story all over the media and entertainment news. She couldn't remember the number of talk shows she and Marshall had been invited to. They were supposed to be promoting the new album they were releasing together. Instead, all the talk show hosts wanted to speak about was them and how Cat felt about Paul's pending divorce.

Cat didn't want to talk about Paul's failed marriage or how it made her feel because she was seeing every country music fan's dream guy, Marshall Myers. She wanted to speak about her new album, which she was so excited about. It featured three duets with her and Marshall, four new solo songs by Cat, and two new solo songs by Marshall. But the album didn't sell as well as they'd anticipated. That was until they eloped a few months after its release and had an eight-month whirlwind romance. Then suddenly the album shot to number two on the charts. Three months after Cat and Marshall had been married, she was working on new material for her next concert tour. Thanks to the success of their duet and his two new songs, which Cat wrote for him, Marshall had also booked a tour. He needed more material, which he asked Cat to write for him because he was supposedly suffering from severe writer's block. But Cat hadn't had time to write his songs. She'd had to concentrate on finishing hers for her new album that coincided with her three-month-long world tour. She also had to find time to record the songs. Marshall had been furious. He'd asked her if he could use some of her new material, but she'd already recorded most of it and was on the last song.

The last was the cover song for her new album, Hearts on Fire, which was also the name of her latest world tour. The song was very dear to her heart and was one she'd been working on with her mother the year her mom had fallen ill. Cat had been twelve at the time and her mother had passed away before they got to finish it. Cat had always meant to finish the song, and had worked on it over the past thirty-eight years. But something always made her shy away from putting the final touches on it. The day Cat had caught her first husband, Paul, cheating on her was the day she'd finished it.

She'd held onto the song, not wanting to release it with the album she'd done with Marshall. It didn't feel right, and Cat had already had plans to put it on her next album, Hearts on Fire. The Hearts on Fire single was due for release the day after the first concert of the tour, which was in London, and the album a week later. Marshall's American tour was set to start two days before Cat was set to leave for the first leg of her worldwide tour. They had only been married for six months, and already their marriage was on the rocks. After Cat refused to write any more material for Marshall, he'd threatened her and told her she'd regret it and then walked out on her. That was the day that Cat knew for sure that she'd never really been in love with Marshall. He'd been her rebound relationship after her divorce from Paul.

Cat had filed for a divorce a few weeks before she was due to leave for the Hearts on Fire World tour. To her delighted surprise Marshall had signed the divorce without any issues or having to meet with their lawyers. He'd accepted that he left the marriage with what he came into it or what he'd bought or contributed to while they were married. Marshall couldn't lay claim to any of Cat's music or revenue from it either. Cat had been so pleased to have had West talk her into making Marshall sign a prenup before they married. Especially after she arrived in London to start her tour and her troubles with Marshall Myers began. It was also the day Cat found out why so many people had warned her against getting involved with the man in the first place. Marshall turned out to be every bit of a snake everyone had said he was.

The sad thing about Marshall was that he was a really gifted singer. But he was lazy and far too arrogant. Marshall also had a lot of problems that Cat had only become aware of two days after she'd arrived in London. She'd been excited to be back in London and to finally sing Hearts on Fire for all her fans to hear. Cat had been doing the final stage and sound check when her assistant told her that West had arrived, but he was not alone. Her lawyer was him along with the head of the PR company that represented her. The moment she'd heard that they were with West, Cat knew something was wrong. Every nerve end in her body had started to zing with tiny electric shock waves.

Cat never read the tabloids. All she ever watched on television were some shows she enjoyed and the news. But over the past few days, Cat had been rehearsing and getting ready for her first concert, so she hadn't had the time to watch television. Her media assistant handled all her social media accounts for her. Cat hated all the hype, but it was good for her image, so she had to have a social media presence. She hardly ever looked at any of them, especially when she knew how it could affect an artist. Cat had worked hard on keeping her image clean. Right up until her second divorce she'd had an untarnished name for thirty years. But all that changed thanks to that lying snake Marshal Myers.

A noise outside the house caught Cat's attention and drew her from her thoughts. She walked to the front door and pulled it open. Cat's son, Indy, and his cousin, Liam were helping Zac up the front stairs.

"You're here." Zac gave her a pained smile.

"I promised your son and daughter I would be," Cat reminded him. "I've made up the room Jamie wanted me to get you settled in."

"I knew I should've invested in a chair lift for the stairs," Zac grumbled, hobbling slowly along on his crutches. "These darn crutches hurt my sore ribs."

"I told you it would've been easier in a wheelchair," Liam pointed out.

"What were you and Indy going to do?" Zac looked at Liam. "Pick me up in the wheelchair and carry it up the front stairs?"

"Yes," Indy said. "I was the one who lifted you onto the stretcher for the helicopter."

"Yes, but now I'm weighed down by a cast on my leg." Zac looked down at his leg. "I'm stuck like this for four to six weeks."

"Or more if you don't heed your other doctor's advice and mine," Liam warned him. "You have to keep off your feet as much as possible."

"Yeah, yeah," Zac sighed. "I know. I have to balance rest with light exercise."

"I'll be here as much as I can during the day," Cat promised. "Don't worry, I'll make sure he does what he's been told to."

"Let's get you to bed," Liam said.

"I don't want to go to bed," Zac argued. "I've been in one for days now."

"The only reason you were signed out was on the condition that you stay in bed for at least the first two days," Liam reminded him. "When I'm not on rotation at the hospital I'll come and relieve Aunt Cat."

"Great, another prison guard," Zac mumbled reluctantly, walking into the ground floor bedroom.

"Do you want anything to eat or drink?" Cat asked him.

"Not just yet, thank you, Cat," Zac said. "I think I'll take a little nap. I woke up extra early this morning and had hardly any sleep last night."

"If you're in pain I do have medication to leave with Cat," Liam told him.

"Thanks, Liam, but I'm fine for now," Zac assured him. "The hospital gave me an injection just before we left to come home so I wouldn't feel the road too much."

"I'll leave you to get dressed and settled," Cat said. "I'll be back as soon as you're in bed with some chamomile tea, which will help you sleep."

"That would be nice," Zac smiled in appreciation. "Please put lots of honey in it with a dash of..."

"Mint." Cat laughed. "I remember how you like to drink tea."

"I was just making sure." Zac grinned back.

Zac's eyes looked heavy with fatigue. Cat knew he was downplaying just how tired his injuries were making him, and the exertion of the travel home was wearing on him.

"I'll be back shortly." Cat turned and left the room, heading for the kitchen.

As she entered the kitchen, her heart jolted with fright when she saw the back of a tall, broad-shouldered man looking in the refrigerator. When he turned around, her heart skipped a few beats as her eyes met the warm hazel ones of David Miller's.

"Hi," David gave her a smile that made his face light up. "Sorry, I didn't mean to startle you."

"Hi," was all Cat could manage right then.

"I heard you mention tea, so I came and put the kettle on," David explained. "I drove Zac home from the hospital and brought his bag in. There were too many people in his room already, so I thought I'd make myself useful and start the tea."

"Thank you," Cat said. "That was thoughtful of you, and thank you for bringing my brother home."

"Of course." David's brow furrowed. "That's what good friends do."

"Can I make you some tea or coffee?" Cat spurred herself on and walked further into the kitchen, where she found David had already got the cups out.

"I'll have a cup of coffee," David said. "Instant will do me just fine."

Cat nodded and busied herself finishing the beverage preparations. "Do you know if Zac has any cookies?" She started going through the kitchen cupboards. "I know he must have some because he loves them."

"Yes, he does." David walked over to one of the kitchen cupboards and showed her. "You have quite the selection."

Cat's eyes widened when she peeked into what turned out to

be a cupboard just for Zac's favorite cookies. "Good grief!" she breathed. "I thought maybe his habit would lessen over time, but it seems to have got a lot worse."

"Jamie and Hayden are constantly on at him about his sweet tooth." David laughed. "But Zac ignores them and says it's his one vice in life. Everyone is allowed one."

"Yes, that's what my father always used to say when I'd have a go at him about his sweets." Cat shook her head.

She chose a few different types of cookies and laid them out on a plate. The kettle started to whistle, and she finished making the beverages.

"I hope this is okay?" Cat handed David his coffee.

As he took the cup their fingers touched and a bolt of lightning shot up Cat's arm straight to her heart, awakening the excitement fluttering in her belly. She'd gotten such a shock at the reaction to that light touch that she'd nearly dropped the cup before David had fully grasped it. Cat had to force herself not to yank her hand away.

"Can I help you with the tray?" David asked her.

"No thanks," Cat said. "I should be fine, and Zac should be in bed by now."

"Lead the way." David stepped aside and let Cat walk ahead of him.

When they got to Zac's bedroom door, David stepped around her, knocked, waited for a reply, and then opened the door for her.

"Cookies!" Zac said in delight. "I've missed my coffee and cookies." He sighed.

"Well, you have the cookies part," Cat told him. "The coffee is for another day."

David, Liam, and Indy pulled up some chairs next to Zac's bed while Cat served up the drinks.

"Did you find out if the water was poisoned?" Cat asked Liam.

"We did," Liam said. "There's nothing in the water."

"Then what killed the deer?" Zac looked at Liam. Cat could see he was struggling to keep his eyes open.

"We're still not sure, Uncle Zac," Indy said. "I've called in a friend of mine to come take some samples of the ground as well as the foliage around there."

"Take your friend to where some of the cattle died as well," Zac told him.

"I will," Indy assured him.

"Good." Zac nodded. "The sooner we get that done the better. We need to figure this out. So many heads of cattle and other animals have died over the past few years."

"Really?" Cat frowned, looking at Zac.

"Yes." Zac nodded, closed his eyes, and pinched the bridge of his nose. "At first, it was Four Lakes ranch that was the worst hit, but then it rolled through to all of us surrounding them."

"There's also been a lot of poaching going on in the woods that surround the five ranches." David leaned forward to look at her. "There's also been a significant decline in the wild horses that roam the area."

"Quite a few of those horses have also gotten ill with some disease that started to spread through the area like a wildfire," Liam told Cat. "My Uncle Brett lost three of his prize quarter horses."

"Mountain Rise lost two of their prize horses, Four Lakes lost a whole lot more, as did Double A Ranch." David shook his head. "These past five years have been the hardest for Cupid's Bow Ranch and the four ranches surrounding it."

"Why am I only hearing about this now?" Cat said, alarmed at what she was hearing.

"Cat, you've been busy with your own life, and I didn't want to burden you with all this." Zac smiled at her. "Besides, you were the one that kept all of us going when we hit the worst patch." He stifled yet another yawn.

"If I knew what was going on I could've done a lot more," Cat told him. "When you're feeling better you can catch me up."

She stood up and looked at the three men sitting around his bed pointedly. “Right now, you need to get some rest.”

“Sorry, I am quite tired,” Zac admitted. “Thank you, all of you, for helping me out.”

David, Indy, and Liam said their goodbyes and then left.

“I’ll be in the lounge if you need me,” Cat told him. “I’m going to leave the door open a bit so I can hear you.”

Zac gave her a tired smile. His eyes were closed, and he’d drifted off before she’d left the room.

Chapter Five

THE HOUSES THAT ZAC BUILT

While Zac slept, Cat looked around his house and came across the attic room. He'd replaced the pull-down stairs with permanent ones. Curious, Cat climbed them. She'd never really liked attics. They creeped her out, and she was petrified of being locked in one. Plus, she'd seen far too many disturbing movies about them. But this one looked like it had a lot of natural light. When she walked into the room, she was impressed. Zac had turned the attic into his office. Her brother had always been compulsively organized, and nothing had changed, Cat noted, eyeing out the filing system. Even his desk was neat.

Cat smiled and walked over to the large antique desk that had belonged to their father. Zac had even restored their father's old office chair. Cat sat down behind the desk in it and looked up at the windows that lined the roof. There was a row on both sides of the ceiling that ran down the attic. Cat had noticed when she walked up to their ranch house that Zac had put similar windows in the attic there. He must've converted their old attic into rooms for the inn. That thought made Cat frown, wondering what Zac must've done with all their mother's and father's things that were stored up there.

Her hand immediately went to the necklace she always wore

around her neck, and she pulled it out from beneath her shirt. It was a gold pendant with an intricate design and a medium-sized ruby in the center. Cat's father had given her the necklace on her eighteenth birthday, and it was one of the last gifts he'd given her before he'd died a few days later. It had belonged to his mother, who'd handed it down to him, then it had been handed down to her. Cat's mother had always worn it and Cat had always assumed that it had belonged to her mother. She'd been surprised to learn that it was a Sparrow family heirloom.

The necklace had a bit of history. Her father had told her that one day it would unlock their past, helping her to understand the Sparrow family. So, she would know the responsibility they have to the land around them and the people who live on it. Her father hadn't had time to explain it any further. Cat's birthday dinner had been cut short by a fire that had broken out on the Double A Ranch which bordered Cupid's Bow. The Andersons who owned the ranch needed help. Cat's father had promised to continue the discussion another day, but that day never came because he died a few days later. She had been so shell-shocked by his unexpected death that the conversation was forgotten.

Cat had looked at the necklace many times over the years and wondered about its strange design. But she'd never let herself reflect on that talk she and her father had. Because even after thirty-two years, his death still stung and brought up too many questions. Cat knew without a shadow of a doubt that Callum's death had not been an accident. Too many things just hadn't added up. Cat's stepmother had deemed it an accident and the case had been closed, but Cat had managed to convince the coroner at the local morgue to do an autopsy on her father. The coroner was also a good friend of her father's.

When he'd given Cat the results of the autopsy, it was in a sealed envelope. He'd warned Cat that opening it wouldn't bring her father back, and that some things were best left alone. That warning had rung in her head the whole way home with that envelope sitting on the seat beside her. Although she was tempted to rip it open and find out the truth, something stopped her. It was like every instinct in her body screamed at her not to. For some reason, she knew that nothing good would come of her digging into her father's death. That doing so would open a door to a journey that would not end well for a lot of people she loved. It would also probably refuel the generations-old feud between the five bordering farms. A feud that her generation had managed to call a truce to, albeit a rather shaky one.

What Cat did know was that the attic in their family home had contained a trunk loaded with answers and Sparrow history that she and her brother would one day need. And Cat had a feeling that they were going to need that information in the very near future. She held the pendant at eye level. Cat's pendant apparently held some of the answers too. Hopefully, when the time came, she'd understand how exactly this piece of jewelry was going to unlock those secrets and answers. Cat's eyes scanned the room but there were none of the old chests or things from the ranch's attic. She made a mental note to ask Zac where he'd stored them. The attic items also held a lot of their memories, so hopefully, he'd not thrown anything out. Cat had also stored a few things up there, including a trunk with their father's autopsy report she'd never opened.

Thinking about her father's autopsy document made her think of another document she'd received from the hospital. It was the results from some tests Cat had asked to be run a few weeks before she'd left home thirty-one years ago. That envelope also remained unopened, and she'd stored it with her father's results. The tests she'd asked to be run Cat had left unopened because she'd felt so guilty for having them done. But like the autopsy results, Cat had known that one day she and her brother may need them. So, she'd stored them somewhere safe to wait for the appropriate time. Then, time had marched on, and Cat had put them out of her mind. But it was back on her mind now, and Cat needed to find where all the attic stuff was. She stood up and made her way back down the stairs to the living room and was once again startled by David in the kitchen. Cat saw that she'd startled him as well because she watched him quickly close whatever he was looking at.

"Cat!" David laughed and jokingly grabbed his chest. "You nearly scared me to death." He held up the little activities booklet. "I was just looking at this."

"Oh," Cat said, still a little suspicious. "Sally at the reception desk gave that to me to look over all the activities the inn offers."

"I was just remembering how Zac and I planned all these activities," David told her.

"Did you want something?" Cat asked him, not too comfortable with the fact that David just walked into Zac's house whenever he wanted.

"I was just getting a bottle of water before heading up to the office," David explained.

"Zac's office upstairs?" Cat's brows furrowed once again.

"Yes, Sally, who doubles as Zac's assistant, and I use the office upstairs for all the back office stuff for the ranch as well as the inn." David walked over to the refrigerator. "Would you like a bottle of water?"

"No thank you," Cat said. That explained the extra desks and landlines in the attic. "I was just looking at how Zac had converted his attic into an office."

"Yes, it seemed a lot more cost-effective than building a whole new structure," David told her. "Zac wants to put stairs leading from the side of the house up to the attic, so we don't have to troop through his house. Which will be great for any business customers as well."

"That seems like a good idea." Cat walked into the kitchen and picked up her pamphlet.

There was something about the way he'd looked at her when she'd caught him reading it that had made her suspicions rise. She opened the booklet and the page immediately opened to Sally's message to her. The note had been flipped upside down, and Cat knew that's not how she'd put it back in the book. Little alarm bells started to ring in her head, and she shook them off. Cat put her suspicions down to her abject mistrust of people that she'd developed over the past four years.

"Indy is drawing up the plans for Zac," David said, and then looked at his watch. "I have an online meeting in twenty minutes, and I need to get prepared." He smiled at her and started walking toward the stairs. "If you need anything, just let me know."

"Thank you," Cat said, watching him go.

She shuddered, thinking about people constantly walking in and out of her private residence. Cat made a mental note to ask Indy about Zac's office and the plans to make his home private. She hated the thought of Zac's staff being able to access his house whenever they pleased. Her brother had no privacy at the moment. Cat lived in a fishbowl since she'd become a successful and famous country singer. Her life was constantly monitored by her fans and reporters. But she guarded her private home life like a fierce lioness with cubs. She showed the public only what she felt they needed to know. The rest was hers, her family's, and close friends' business. One of the reasons that she never came home was in case she was followed, or at least that was her excuse.

Cat Sparrow's origins had remained a mystery since her first number one smash hit. All the public knew was that she grew up in Montana. Thank goodness she'd done that, and that Marshall had never found out where she was really from. Because Cat knew Lewistown, Montana would've become a hotbed for every gossip-hungry reporter. Not to mention the angry Marshall Myers mob of fans that were out for her blood. She shuddered again, thinking about how her beautiful Brentwood home had been trashed by his fans. Cat was also still furious that her address had been leaked after all these years. She took a deep breath to calm herself as the anger started to rise inside her at the thought of what had happened that had made her have to retreat to her home in Montana.

Her manager, West Lockran, and PR manager, Pat Healy

were planning on joining in a week's time to discuss her way forward. Her bodyguard, Wallace Black, was due to arrive in Montana tomorrow. Cat had wanted Wallace to stay in Brentwood and make sure there were no more attacks on her home. But West had insisted Wallace be with her in Montana in case the press and angry fans got wind of where she was. While she couldn't argue with West's logic, it had been nice to be able to do her own thing without her constant shadow. Although Cat had to admit to being so grateful for Wallace when her troubles began. The man was a highly trained ex-marine that knew how to make a person disappear in plain sight. Something Cat had needed to do when she had almost been mobbed by a very angry crowd of Marshal Myers fans.

Cat shook off her gloomy thoughts. Now was not the time to brood over her second ex-husband and how he'd exploited her perfect life. Cat had seen many celebrities become victims of angry fans and sadistic reporters. She'd always felt sorry for them at how quickly they could fall from the public's grace. Now here she was, tumbling down the stardom ladder fast on her way to rock bottom and tomorrow's news. Anger bubbled up inside her once again. But she was determined to climb right back up and knock the person who should be falling off the top rung. Cat had worked hard to get where she was and develop her reputation to let some lying, cheating weasel do this to her. She took another deep breath to calm herself again, closed her eyes, and tried to think of something else. Her brother, son, Cupids Bow Ranch, and the four ranches that surrounded Cupids Bow needed all the help they could get right now, it seemed. Cat was glad to have the distraction from her own problems to see where she could help.

"Cat?" Zac's call got her attention.

Cat put the booklet Sally had given her into her purse and hid her purse in one of the lower kitchen cupboards. She knew she was being paranoid, but there was still just something about the way David had looked when she'd walked into the kitchen that troubled her. In fact, she wondered just how well her brother actually knew David. Cat knew that they had gone to college and the army together. But she wondered if Zac knew anything about David's family or where he was originally from.

"Cat!" Zac called once again.

"Coming," Cat said, walking towards his bedroom. "Hi, are you okay?"

Cat walked into Zac's room where he was trying to pull himself into a sitting position.

"Here, let me help you," Cat said.

Jamie had ordered a special orthopedic bed for Zac. It allowed for slings that they could use to raise his leg, and it also hung a drip if needed. It also adjusted as the hospital beds did, so Cat raised the side by Zac's head until he was in a sitting position.

"Is that better?" Cat smiled.

"Thank you," Zac said. Cat could hear the frustration in his voice. "I hate feeling like an invalid."

"You're not an invalid," Cat told him. "You're injured. There's a big difference."

"It's just so frustrating. I have so much to do," Zac moaned.

"I know," Cat said patiently. "But I'm here and available to help you with whatever you need. So put me to work."

"It has a lot to do with the inn and running the ranch," Zac told her. "Do you even remember how to run a ranch?" He gave her a cheeky grin.

"Of course, I do." Cat laughed. "Daddy started teaching us both how to run the place before we could walk properly."

"Good, then you don't mind overseeing some of the day-to-day ranch operations?" Zac asked her. "There's not that much you'd have to do because David is a really good foreman, but there are things only us Sparrows can take care of."

"Not a problem," Cat assured Zac. "You tell me what you need me to do."

"You're going to need a notepad and pen," Zac told her.

"Okay," Cat said. "Will I find that in your office?"

"I see you've been looking around my house." Zac smiled. "What do you think?"

"It's amazing," Cat told him honestly. "David told me about the staircase you want to put in for office access. I think that should be made a priority."

"Yes, Indy is working on the plans," Zac told her.

"David said so." Cat nodded. "I see you built six of these houses. It's like a little neighborhood within Cupids Bow."

"I built one for each of us," Zac explained. "You know how much I like having my family close to me."

"I know," Cat told him. "It was also daddy's dream to have us kids live close to him. If I remember correctly, he was going to build housing like this."

"That's right," Zac confirmed. "I found the plans he'd drawn up for this little development."

"Oh?" Cat was surprised by that revelation. "I didn't realize daddy had actually gone as far as planning the development."

"I thought it would be a great way to honor him," Zac told her. "Did you see the name of the little street I've put in?"

"No," Cat shook her head.

"Callum Drive," Zac said.

"That's beautiful, Zac." Cat swallowed the tears. "I know Daddy would've approved."

"Indy has already moved into his house." Zac looked at Cat. "You should go and have a look. He has the keys to the house I built for you."

"I will do that," Cat promised. "But right now, let me go get a pen and notebook so I can list my ranch duties."

"Okay, would you mind bringing me some more water, please?" Zac asked her. "I've finished the bottles you put here before."

"My goodness, Zac." Cat looked at the empty water bottles. "I'll bring you some refills."

Cat took the empty water bottles to put in the recycling bin and went in search of stationery.

Cat was about to walk up the stairs to Zac's office when she stopped because she could hear David talking to someone. He sounded rather angry. Cat quietly crept a little higher up the stairs, stopping where she would still be out of sight. She knew it was rude to eavesdrop, but Cat's suspicion of David had been raised, and this time she was listening to her instincts.

"I told you not to call me here!" David hissed. "No, I have not, and I told you this was a lengthy process." There was a pause. "I know it's already been over ten years, but you've been here a lot longer than that now and what have you accomplished?" There was another pause. "I'm also going to warn you once again that I'd better not find out that you or any of your associates are responsible for everything."

Cat felt shock waves zing through her nervous system when she heard that.

Is he referring to the trouble that's been happening on all the ranches in the area? Cat wondered. She made a mental note to ask Zac how long David had been working at Cupids Bow. Now her suspicions of David had grown even more. What was he up to? Then another thought struck her. What if he wasn't who he said he was either? Cat's heart started to hammer in her chest. Thoughts of her first meeting with David thirty-two years ago flashed through her head.

Cat had met David the day of her father, Callum Sparrow's, funeral thirty-two years ago. She'd been so overwhelmed by her father's death and the people crowding her house that she'd retreated to the stables. But once she was there, she'd seen the horse that her father had supposedly had his accident on, and everything had suddenly become too much for her. Cat had taken off at a sprint, not really knowing where she was going until David had caught up with her and calmed her down. Then they'd spent hours just sitting in the field where he'd let her cry on his shoulder. Other than having met in the stable before Cat had taken off on her run, she hadn't met him. She'd known that her brother had a friend coming to visit and stay with them, but they hadn't been introduced. Cat hadn't realized that David had arrived the day of the funeral and she may even have been introduced to him. But a lot about that day had been a big blur to Cat.

What Cat had remembered most about that day had been how safe she'd felt around David. He was so calm, compassionate, and understanding that he'd made her regain some of her sanity, allowing her to re-anchor herself to her whirling world. When all the emotions inside of her had bubbled out and settled, that's when other emotions had surfaced. But Cat hadn't had time to explore them, nor did she want to. David had been a complete stranger and she'd put what she'd thought was love at first sight down to transference. Cat had been feeling vulnerable and just lost a man that meant the world to her, and she was looking to fill that gap. David had been kind, caring, and patient to a complete stranger in a vulnerable state. It was only natural that she felt an infatuation for him.

Cat hadn't seen David again after that day. Zac had left to go back to university the night of their father's funeral, taking David with him. The next time Cat had seen David again was a few days ago when she'd arrived back in Montana. Maria had sent him to fetch her from the Billings airport. Cat was no longer a trusting naive girl. After two divorces she realized you never really knew anyone as well as you thought you did. People were masters of deception, and Cat was no better. She too held back parts of her, but she never cheated or tried to break anyone down like Marshall Myers was doing to her.

A noise from the office yanked Cat from her deep thoughts, and she realized she was still standing on the stairs. She made some jumping noises on the stairs as if she was running up them, and popped up into the office.

"Oh, hi," David said with a big smile. "Is everything okay with Zac?"

"Yes." Cat nodded, trying to act as calmly as possible so he wouldn't know she'd been listening to his conversation. "Zac asked me to get a pen and notepad."

"Of course." David stood up from his desk and walked over to one of the cupboards on the far end of the room. He pulled out a pen and book. "Here you go."

David walked back towards her and handed her the items.

"Thank you." Cat took them from him.

"Is Zac already writing up to-do lists for me?" David gave a soft laugh.

"No," Cat said. "I'm taking down notes so I can step in for him while he's laid up."

"Oh!" David said, looking surprised. "Are you going to be able to handle filling in for him?"

"Why?" Cat instantly went on the defensive at his words. "Don't you think a woman can run a ranch?"

"What?" David looked at her stunned for a second. "No, that's not what I meant at all. But you don't have experience running a ranch."

"Excuse me?" Cat's eyes narrowed. "You don't know anything about me or what I'm capable of."

"I know." David held up his hands. "I'm sorry, that's not what I meant at all." His eyes widened and he shook his head. "Sorry, everything I say is coming out wrong here. Can I start over?" He gave her a boyish grin.

"No, don't bother," Cat said. "I think you've said quite enough already." Her eyes narrowed even more. "But know this, while I am stepping in for Zac, I intend to go over everything about the ranch that I need to know." She warned him. "I'll expect you to be around when I need the answers I can't find. I'll also want to do a ride over the ranch in the next few days. We'll divide it into sections to do them one day at a time due to the size of *my* land."

"Yes," David said without hesitation. "Of course, whatever you need." He looked at her. "I'll even choose a horse for you."

"No need," Cat told him. "Mine is arriving this afternoon and will need a good run."

"Okay." David looked at her. "I wasn't told about any horses arriving today, but I can organize a stable for your horse immediately."

"Once again, there's no need," Cat said. "My horse won't be stabled here."

"Are you keeping it at Big Valley Ranch with Maria?" David asked.

"Yes." Cat nodded. "Now if you'll excuse me, I need to go talk to my brother."

David gave her a slight bow and stepped out of her way.

Chapter Six

A COLLECTION OF HORSES

David's eyes narrowed as he watched Cat turn and flounce out of the room. He'd got a shock when Zac told him that Cat was coming home for a while. She was a complication that David did not need in his life at the moment. He'd been relieved when he'd heard that she'd be staying with the Parkers at Big Valley Ranch rather than Cupids Bow. David had come too far now to have anything get in the way of his goals. But now that Cat was back, nosing around at Cupids Bow, he had a feeling things may not go as smoothly as he'd planned.

When David had found out that Cat was coming back home, he'd immediately got suspicious as to why. He was suspicious by nature, and his being so close to achieving what he came here for coinciding with her arriving home was a little too coincidental for him. As was Zac's accident that would set the last bit of establishing the inn back at least a few weeks, which meant David's plans would also have to be knocked back. At first, he'd been disappointed in having to put his plans back once again. But it gave him a bit more time on the ranch, and Cat being home could give him access to her house. It was the only house that had been locked up tighter than Fort Knox on the ranch. David wanted to know why.

David turned to look out of the ceiling-to-floor one-way glass window Zac had installed in the attic office. He'd said that he liked the light. David had a feeling that there was more to it than that as the window looked out onto the house he'd built for Cat. Then there were all the cameras Zac had installed around the ranch. After what had been happening to all the ranches, most of the owners had been doing the same. But there were a lot more cameras and security systems installed in and around the house Zac had built for Cat on the ranch. Zac was also the only one allowed in the house, and he even supervised the cleaning crew twice a week. David had tried to question one of the cleaning crew, but he couldn't get any answers from them. They were as tight-lipped about the house as the house was secured.

That had only raised David's curiosity more as he wondered what Zac was hiding in the house. The one time he'd questioned Zac about it, Zac had said it was because of Cat being a celebrity, but once again David knew he'd been lying. There was a lot more going on with that house, and David wanted to know what it was. A commotion from outside caught his attention. He stood up and walked to the window where he saw Janine, the inn's manager, running after a tall man with broad shoulders. His face was hidden by his black Stetson. His stride and the way he carried his frame told David the man meant business.

David opened the window slightly and he could hear the conversation between the man and Janine.

"Sir, I told you, you can't just come back here, these are private residences for the owner and his family," Janine said, sounding breathless as she tried to keep up with the man's long stride. "If you don't stop and go back to the main inn this instance, you'll give me no choice but to call the police."

"Go ahead," the man's voice was controlled, but he didn't stop striding towards the house.

"Fine!" Janine stopped walking right before she got to Zac's front gate and pulled out her phone.

David's eyes narrowed as he watched the man walk through the gate, and he lost sight of him when he got to the front steps.

David turned and rushed out of the office to go and find out just who the man was.

Before he was at the bottom of the stairs leading to the ground floor, the man was knocking at the door and Cat beat David to it.

"I've got it," Cat glanced back at David as she headed for the front door.

David stopped on the bottom stair and nodded. Cat pulled the door open, and David froze when he saw the man standing there.

No! It couldn't be! David stood frozen to the spot for a second before he walked back up the stairs and out of view of the front door so he could observe. David watched Cat's posture instantly relax when she saw the man. *Does Cat know him?*

"Wallace!" Cat breathed in relief. "I'm so glad you're here."

"Well, that's the first time you've been glad to see me," Wallace said.

"Cat, I'm so sorry about..." Janine rushed up behind Wallace. "You know this man?"

"I do," Cat told Janine. "Janine, this is Wallace Black and you'll be seeing him around here a lot."

"Oh!" Janine's eyes widened. "I wish you would've told me you were expecting a guest." She looked at Wallace awkwardly. "I apologize for my rudeness."

"You were doing your job," Wallace excused her.

"How is Zac?" Janine asked Cat.

"Do you want to go see him?" Cat asked her.

"I don't want to disturb him if he's resting," Janine said.

"No, he's just being grouchy and wanting to get up," Cat told her. "Go on through."

"Thank you." Janine pushed herself past Wallace, who was blocking the doorway.

"Come inside, Wallace," Cat stepped aside. "I'll introduce you to my brother."

Before David could be seen he quietly went back up the stairs, careful as to not draw Wallace Black's attention, although

David had a suspicion the man knew he was there. He needed to think. Wallace Black was a huge complication that could just unravel everything David had been working for. Because Wallace Black wasn't just any bodyguard. David was sure that the man would've done extensive research on everyone at Cupids Bow Ranch as well as all the ranches in the area. Yes, Wallace Black was trouble with a capital T!

Cat was glad Wallace was there. He could help her with some investigating into what was going on in the area and the alleged animal poisonings. Cat also wanted him to get her some answers about David Miller. There was just something that didn't sit right with her about him. She led Wallace to Zac's room, knocked on the door, waited for a response, and then walked in.

Janine was sitting next to the bed, taking notes on the notepad Cat had left beside Zac's nightstand.

"Zac, this is Wallace, my bodyguard," Cat introduced them.

Zac surprised her by saying, "I know Wallace. Hey, how are you?"

"Zac," Wallace shook his hand. "You're not looking too good, buddy."

"Had a bit of a run-in with a thug, slipped, and knocked myself out." Zac laughed.

"Ouch," Wallace winced. "That's both physically painful and bruising to the ego."

"Tell me about it." Zac sighed.

"Wait a minute," Cat finally found her voice after the shock she got from finding out Wallace and Zac knew each other. "How do you two know each other?"

"We were in the marines together," Zac explained. "Wallace was the one who saved my life when I got injured."

"Why didn't you say anything?" Cat's eyes narrowed when she looked at Wallace.

"I didn't want it to make a difference to whether you hired me or not," Wallace told her. "I prefer to get employed on my credentials rather than my heroics."

"You still should've told me you knew my brother!" Cat raised her eyebrows. "I don't like things like this being kept from me."

"I apologize," Wallace said. "To be fair, you and I never really had any conversations, so I never got a chance to tell you."

"The interview would've been the best place," Cat said.

"Cat, give him a break." Zac shook his head. "Wallace was right not to tell you. You hired him because he was the best man for the job. Not because he knew me or saved my life."

"Is there anything else I should know?" Cat asked.

"Excuse me," Janine said. "But I need to get back to work." She looked at Zac. "Is there anything else you need me to do?"

"No, thanks, Janine." Zac smiled.

"Great, then I'm going to let you three work this out." Janine gave them all a small smile before slipping out of the room.

"Well, is there?" Cat looked from Zac to Wallace.

"Nope," Zac said, shaking his head. "Not on my side."

"Or mine," Wallace assured her.

"Good, because I have something I need you to do for me, please, Wallace," Cat told him. "Zac, will you excuse us? This is just about my horse."

"You want Wallace to look after your horse?" Zac looked at her amazed.

"I told you, I grew up on a ranch," Wallace reminded Zac. "I happen to be very good with horses, and Cat's horse needs extra care."

"Yes, I believe Magenta is as impossible to handle as her father, Zeus, was," Zac said.

"Zeus wasn't impossible," Cat defended her previous horse. "He was just fussy about who handled him."

"Or rode him or came near him," Zac pointed out. "You don't know how many of the stable hands he bit or tried to bite."

"At least he stopped trying to stomp them or kick them." Cat gave Zac a cheeky smile. "Now you need to get some rest. Indy is coming around in an hour and said he'd get you out and about for a while."

"Great," Zac said. "I love being walked like a puppy."

"You're lucky you're getting out at all," Cat told him. "We could've left you in the hospital to recover."

Zac sighed again and shook his head before lying back against his pillows and closing his eyes.

Cat and Wallace quietly left the room.

"Let's go for a walk," Cat suggested. "I'll show you around the stables."

"I'd like that," Wallace said, glancing at the stairs. "Is there someone else in the house?" he asked her softly and Cat nodded, leading him out the front door.

They walked away from the houses and towards the stables.

"I wanted to see my brother's horses anyway," Cat told him. "He has some Arabians and an Akhal-Teke."

"Yes, I believe Zac got lucky with that horse," Wallace said, following Cat to the main stables.

"Wow, he has changed this place." Cat stood staring in amazement at the new stables. "Let's go find our way around."

"These stables remind me a lot of my father's," Wallace told her.

"I believe that Zac asked my son to model them off a breeder that was selling his ranch." Cat walked to the first stable. "Hey, there."

A roan quarter horse whinnied and stuck its head over the stall door for some affection.

"You're a friendly one, aren't you?" Wallace laughed, making Cat turn and stare at him in amazement. "What?" Wallace's brow instantly creased when he saw her look.

"Oh, I've never heard you laugh before," Cat pointed out.

"I've laughed," Wallace said.

"No, that was a natural heartfelt laugh," Cat told him.

"I didn't realize there were different kinds of laughs." Wallace raised his eyebrows.

He was soon laughing again when the horse stuck its wet nose against Wallace's face for more attention.

"You really love horses, don't you?" Cat looked at him.

"Guilty," Wallace admitted. "They're the most intuitive creatures around. The Native American culture viewed them as spiritual figures. Some people believe horses can see into your soul."

"My father used to say that." Cat's voice grew hoarse thinking about her father.

"So did mine." Wallace's eyes became shadowed. "Where does Zac keep his Arabians and the Akhal-Teke?"

"You, know I'm not sure, but I think that man over there," Cat pointed to one of the stable hands that was walking towards them, "can help us."

"Hello." The man walked up to them. "Can I ...." His eyes grew wide. "You're Cat Sparrow. Zac's sister?"

"Yes." Cat nodded. "And you must've been employed here after I left the ranch."

"Right, I've only been working in these stables for three years," the man told her. "Are you looking for horses to ride?" He turned and pointed towards the open back end of the stables. "The guests' horses are in the next stable down. These are the stables for the quarter horses."

"We were actually looking for the stable where Zac keeps his Arabians and Monarch," Cat told him.

"Oh." The man nodded. "You want the palace."

"The palace?" Cat frowned.

"That's what we call the stables where Zac's prize horses are kept," the man informed them. "Come, I'll show you."

The man turned and started walking towards where the arena used to be. Cat stopped when she saw him turning towards it.

"Isn't that the indoor arena?" Cat asked him.

"Oh, no," the man shook his head. "There is a whole new building out the back that houses the arenas."

"Arenas?" Cat's frown deepened.

"Yes," the man said. "Why don't I give you a tour of the stable complex?"

"We'd like that," Wallace told him.

"Sorry, I didn't get your name," Cat said to the man.

"I'm Craig," the man introduced himself. "Sorry, my manners flew out the window there." He laughed nervously. "You'd think we didn't get celebrities in here."

"You're the second person to mention celebrities visiting the ranch." Cat looked at Craig curiously.

"I don't know if you know Simone Clark?" Craig asked them.

"I do," Cat informed him.

"She stayed here many times over the years to support Zac's efforts to save the ranch," Craig told her. "Through her word of mouth about how discreet and wonderful the ranch inn was, the celebrity presence started to grow."

"I didn't know that," Cat said, surprised.

"Monarch, Mystique, Caesar, and Rio live here." Craig pushed the door open to where the indoor arena once was.

Cat froze at the door. Her heart started to accelerate. *Good grief, Cat!* She admonished herself, trying to swallow down the horrible feeling of dread in the pit of her stomach. *It's been nearly thirty-two years since daddy died!*

"Are you okay?" Wallace said quietly. "You look like you've seen a ghost."

"That's where my father died," Cat managed to say.

"We don't have to go in there," Wallace told her patiently.

"No," Cat swallowed again and took a deep breath, "I really think I do."

"Okay." Wallace stepped back and let her go through before him. "I'm right behind you."

"Thank you," Cat whispered and forced herself to walk into the room.

Cat's eyes widened in shock when she saw what Zac had done to their old arena. There were eight stables much like the others, but each of these stables had digital monitors on the doors. The monitor had the name of the horse and the screens switched with information every few minutes. It listed the horse's health, name, feeding time, exercise time, and more.

"Zac has horse monitoring systems now?" Cat looked at Craig in amazement.

"Yes," Craig confirmed. "These horses have. He wants to get them for all the horses eventually."

"This is amazing." Cat glanced up at the wall above the door frame that led through to another part of the stable.

"Are you okay?" Wallace asked her softly.

"Yes." Cat smiled at him. "I think that Zac changing the place has made it a lot easier to be in here."

"Zac has really done an amazing job with these stables." Wallace looked around.

"That big monitor on the wall," Cat looked at Craig, "it has a lot more than three horses on it."

"That's because that's the central system that lets the stable staff know what horses are where," Craig explained. "There are a lot of horses on the ranch, especially if you include the working quarter horses."

"So, every time a horse is taken out you have to log it?" Cat looked at him.

"Yes," Craig nodded. "All the horses are microchipped because they have to be in order to get them registered." He told them. "We use that to identify each of them and keep track of them. On each of the barn doors is a scanner that reads the chip every time the horse passes through it."

"Wow!" Cat said, impressed.

"If the horse is not authorized to be leaving the stable Zac, David, and I are alerted," Craig explained. "We can also track them thanks to their chips now with this new program that Liam Parker wrote for us."

"Liam writes software?" It was Wallace's turn to be surprised. "I thought he was studying medicine."

"Oh, Liam is a total computer geek," Cat told Wallace. "He's been programming since he was ten."

"Yes, the system he has designed for the ranch is amazing," Craig raved. "Zac is trying to get Liam to put it on the market as he knows he will make a fortune from it. We have already had other stables asking about it."

"I'm currently installing the system at Big Valley Ranch," Liam made Cat jump as he walked up behind them. "Hi, Aunty Cat." He gave her a hug and a kiss.

"Where did you come from?" Cat spun around.

"I was in the stable office," Liam pointed towards what was once the viewing area that sat above the arena.

"Gosh, this place has really changed," Cat said. "I must say I'm impressed with this system you wrote, Liam. Maybe you've missed your calling and you should be a computer software engineer and not a doctor."

"Nah," Liam shook his head. "Programming is my hobby. Being a doctor is my true calling."

"Yes, but your hobby seems to be a very lucrative one," Wallace pointed out.

"We'll see," Liam said. "Between Uncle Zac and Uncle Brett, they are driving me crazy with little things each of them wants to be included for their stables."

"Well, at least you know that it will have a lot to offer to stables if you do want to market the program," Cat told him.

"I guess," Liam shrugged. "Is Craig giving you the grand tour of the stables?"

"He is." Cat smiled at Craig.

"Good, I have to go check on Uncle Zac and then get to the hospital for my shift." Liam looked at his watch. "I'll see you later." He said his goodbyes and rushed off.

"He's always in a rush, that boy." Cat sighed.

"He's a busy young man," Wallace said as they followed Craig through the stables and into an outdoor area that had a few large paddocks.

Craig raised his hands to his lips and whistled. One of the largest horses Cat had ever seen came barreling down the hill. It cleared the first few paddock fences effortlessly like it was stepping over them. It reared up as it got to the fence that separated them from the field before dropping back onto all fours. The beast shook out its golden mane, and its silky sorrel coat glistened in the sun as he snorted at Craig.

"Oh, my word!" Cat felt tiny standing next to the large horse. "How big is he and who is he?"

Craig laughed when the horse whinnied as if it was trying to introduce itself to Cat on cue.

"He's one of your biggest fans," Craig told her.

"Excuse me?" Cat's brow creased into a frown.

"This is Pegasus," Craig introduced the horse to Cat. "He loves your music." He laughed, seeing the look on both Cat and Wallace's faces. "Watch."

Craig pulled out his phone and put one of Cat's songs on. Pegasus's ears twitched and the horse started moving his head from side to side like he was dancing.

"Oh, my goodness!" Cat's eyes widened in amazement. "He's wonderful."

"He is quite the character," Craig told them.

"Is he a Percheron?" Wallace walked up to the horse, who was enjoying Cat's song.

"Yes," Craig confirmed.

"Is Zac wanting to breed Percheron now?" Cat asked.

"He's amazing," Wallace said, totally captivated by the horse. "He must be just over eighteen hands high."

"Yes, and he'll probably get bigger," Craig said. "He's just over four years old."

"That's unbelievable," Cat breathed. "I can't believe he dances to music."

"Oh, not just any music," Craig told her. "Only your music."

"Really?" Cat laughed looking at Craig suspiciously.

"Really!" Craig assured her. "Pegasus came to Cupid's bow a few days after he was foaled. His mother died three hours after giving birth to him."

"That's awful," Cat felt her heart go out to the horse. "How did Zac find out about him?"

"It wasn't Zac who brought him here," Craig told them. "It was Jamie. A friend of hers breeds them as dressage horses, and she told Jamie about him. He wasn't eating and refused a surrogate mother or the bottle." His eyes were filled with compassion. "The owners weren't quite sure what to do with him, so Jamie stepped in and adopted him."

"Another lucky find for my brother and niece." Cat smiled.

"I think both Zac and Jamie have a gift for detecting horses in need," Craig said. "Jamie worked day and night with Pegasus. He didn't get a name until she was sure he was going to make it."

"It's easier that way," Wallace said. "My daddy always said not to name animals if you're not sure they're going to make it when they're born. He said the minute you put a name to the animal you were forming a bond with it and that could be painful."

"Jamie was determined that this horse was going to live," Craig explained. "Two days in and he'd only taken little bits of milk that Jamie had had to force down his throat. One of the stable hands was playing music two stalls down from where Pegasus was. Your song came on, Jamie was there, and the stable hand turned the music up."

"Are you about to tell me that my music saved Pegasus' life?" Cat looked at Craig in disbelief.

"Jamie seems to think so," Craig told her. "She said the foal started to shake his head. At first, she wasn't quite sure what he was doing. But then as the tempo of the song increased, so did his head shaking. That's when she realized he must be dancing."

"No way," Cat laughed.

"It's true," Craig nodded. "Jamie rushed out and asked the stable hand to come with her. They stopped the music and Pegasus became so upset he started whining until they put the song on again."

"That's incredible," Wallace's brow was creased.

"He even took the bottle after that," Craig told them. "Each feeding time, Jamie would bring her phone with her to play songs for him. But he only responded to Cat's music."

"You do have a magical voice after all," Wallace teased her.

"I can't believe this." Cat laughed.

"Why don't you try singing for him," Wallace suggested.

"Seriously?" Cat shook her head. "No, I don't think so."

When she spoke, she noticed Pegasus' ears twitching.

"Give it a try," Craig encouraged her. "Every time you speak, you get his attention like he knows your voice because of your music."

"What stable was he in when Jamie was nursing him?" Cat asked Craig.

"The third one from the door." Craig's words made her freeze and her eyes widened when she looked at him.

"That was King Callum's stable." Cat breathed and swallowed, and a chill crept up her spine.

"Yes, I believe so," Craig said, not noticing how she'd paled when he'd told her that. "Didn't you take King to your farm in Nashville?"

"I did," Cat confirmed. "I used to sing to King and Zeus, my horse; they were stabled next to each other."

"Oh, in the same stable that King Callum was housed in?" It was Craig's turn to look amazed.

"That song you played for Pegasus," Cat told him. "I wrote it for King when he became ill. I used to take my songbook and guitar to go sit in King's stable at night to ensure he made it through."

"The song was written about King Callum," realization dawned on Craig.

"That's why it's called You are the King," Cat smiled. "It was also my first number one hit."

"That's both amazing and scary," Craig told her.

"To think your first number one hit nursed two horses back to health," Wallace said.

"In the same stable," Craig reminded Wallace.

"I'm just glad this beauty lived," Cat stepped up to the huge horse and held out her hand, saying softly, "Hi, Pegasus."

He immediately went to Cat and nose bumped her hand.

"Huh," Craig breathed. "Pegasus likes to nip and did not nose-bump so gently like that." He looked impressed. "I knew he recognized your voice," he said. "The only other person he's so gentle with is Jamie. In fact, I think he's totally in love with her."

Cat carefully lifted her hand and stroked his head, which he lowered for her.

"You are so gorgeous," Cat cooed to Pegasus. "I can see why Jamie rescued you."

"Jamie wants to train him for dressage but he's just turned four so she's waiting a year," Craig told them. "Pegasus' parents are both prize dressage horses."

"Aren't Percheron still used at police and military mounts?" Wallace asked.

"I'm not sure, but Jamie wants to get them back into places like that," Craig explained. "Especially with everyone wanting to go green and petrol prices. She thinks that the police should have more mounted patrols."

"There's nothing more awesome than seeing a mounted police patrol." Cat sighed.

"Percherons were used as war horses way back when," Wallace gave them a bit of history on the breed. "They're very powerful horses."

"They are also incredible in the dressage arena," Cat said. "Which is a much safer environment for them." She laughed when Pegasus bumped her after she'd turned her back on him.

"You have a new best friend, Cat." Wallace laughed.

"It would seem so," Cat agreed with him and pulled an apple from her pocket, which she fed to him.

"Well, if he wasn't your friend before, he is now," Craig assured her. "He loves apples and has no problem stealing them from the other horses' feed sacks."

"You are just the cutest thing, aren't you?" Cat laughed once again when he bobbed his head like he understood what she was saying.

Cool green eyes watched them from afar through binoculars. It was almost time for the next stage of the plan, and he didn't care who the man in the black Stetson with Cat was. If that blasted beast of a horse would move out of the way, they could get a better shot. It was almost as if the horse was purposefully standing in the way. Each time a shot presented itself, the horse moved and blocked the view. A noise caught the shadowy figure's attention. It was time to leave as it was too soon to attract attention. There was still a bit of time. The cool green eyes looked towards the stables one last time before slinking off and blending in with the environment.

Chapter Seven

HALF-TRUTH AND RUNAROUNDS

"If you follow me, I'll introduce you to Caesar, Cupid, and Athena." Craig guided them away from Pegasus and around the stables to another paddock.

There were three horses idly grazing, twitching their ears and turning their heads when they heard Cat, Wallace, and Craig approach. When Cat and Wallace walked up to the fence, two of the horses turned and wandered over to them.

"Hello," Cat said when a black horse with four white dots on her forehead nudged her. "Who are you?"

"That's Glory." Craig scratched the thoroughbred behind the ears. "She's a five-year-old Arabian and the daughter of Caesar and Mystique. She's Jamie's eldest daughter's horse."

"She's beautiful and so friendly," Wallace said, greeting the horse, and then winced when the chestnut mare nipped him on the shoulder. "Hey!" He turned and glared at the mare. "That's not nice."

The horse moved its lips and nodded her head like she was laughing at Wallace.

"That's Sassy," Craig walked over to the mare. "Sassy, you know it's rude to bite our guests." He rubbed Sassy's ears. "She's almost four and is Glory's younger sister, who still needs to learn some manners."

"Hello, Sassy," Wallace made friends with the horse. "Craig is right, biting people is rude."

Sassy whinnied and moved her lips like she was laughing at them again.

"Cheeky!" Wallace laughed.

"I take it they are both the offspring of Mystique and Caesar as well?" Cat asked.

"Yes," Craig nodded. "Sadly, Sassy is the last baby that Mystique will ever have."

"Where is Mystique?" Cat asked.

"The horse standing back there ignoring us is Mystique." Craig pointed to her. "She won't come to you unless she wants to. The only two people who she will actually come to greet on her own accord are Zac and Jamie."

"Horses are such amazing creatures," Cat said. "But Mystique is gorgeous."

"Yes, we call her Queen Mystique because of the way she acts." Craig laughed. "We have Caesar in his stable right now because he's due for a vet check, so I'll take you to him last."

"But I thought you might like to meet Monarch." Craig walked them to another paddock that was quite a distance away from the mares.

When Cat and Wallace rounded the corner, they stopped. Cat's breath caught in her throat when she saw the beautiful horse. He was standing at the fence as if he was waiting for them.

"Hey boy." Craig approached cautiously. "Are you feeling better today?"

"Is he sick?" Cat asked, walking up to the horse.

"Yes, we think he might have eaten something," Craig explained. "All the horses are being checked. I believe Indy's friend is arriving today to check out the grass and soil."

"That's right," Cat said. "I didn't know that Monarch had been infected."

Wallace and Cat approached the stallion with caution, but he just stood there watching them. Cat put her hand up and he nose-bumped it.

"I thought he'd shy away," Cat said, delighted she could touch the horse.

"No, Monarch is not as high-strung as Mystique and Caesar," Craig explained. "He can have his moments of stubbornness where he can be really difficult, though."

"I can imagine." Cat laughed as Monarch tried to get her to scratch him.

"He's just a bit under the weather, but Jamie and the new vet working with her assure us that he's on the mend," Craig told them.

After they left Monarch, Craig took them to see Zac's three thoroughbreds before taking them back into the stables to be introduced to Caesar. He too was a beautiful horse, but he wasn't warming up to strangers.

"That's the tour," Craig told them. "If you need a horse to ride just let me know and I'll organize them for you."

"Thank you, Craig," Cat said.

"If you'll excuse me, I have to get back to work." Craig said his goodbyes and left them.

"Now that we've shaken our tail," Wallace said, "I take it you want me to look into someone or something at Cupids Bow?"

"I do," Cat said. "But what do you mean our tail?"

"Someone was watching up from a distance and another someone was tailing us," Wallace told her. "I'll go see if I can figure out who was watching us, and I have a pretty good idea of who was following us."

"Who?" Cat's eyes widened as she looked at Wallace questioningly.

"Let me find out for definite and I'll let you know," Wallace told her.

"Okay," Cat agreed. "I'd like you to find out what the heck is going on with the ranches. There have been a lot of problems for Cupids Bow and the four ranches that surround us. Things like animals dying and going missing."

"I found out from Maria's brother, Brett Parker, that they've been losing a lot of money," Wallace said. "Brett said that most of them are thinking of turning their ranches into inns like Zac has done to Cupids Bow, just to keep their land."

"The Parkers from Big Mountain Ranch, Anderson's from the Double A, and the Beckett's from Four Lakes have all mortgaged their properties, just to keep them going," Cat explained to him. "They're all hanging on by a thread. But I have a feeling that something is going on."

"It sounds like someone either has a vendetta against the five ranches or ..." Wallace's eyes narrowed when he stopped talking in the middle of his sentence. "Cat, do you know if your brother or any of the other four ranches have received offers to buy their land?"

"I haven't heard anything like that," Cat told him. "Why? Do you think they are being targeted by a development company?"

"I'm not sure yet, but I need to know if any of the ranches have been hounded by someone or a company wanting to buy up land in the area," Wallace told her. "I'll do some digging in the background. I don't want you to ask any questions that will raise suspicions."

"You tell me your theories and then ask me not to nose around?" Cat raised her eyebrows. "Now I'm really curious to find the answers to your questions."

"Yes, but don't try to," Wallace warned her. "Cat, if it is a land developer after the land, some of these companies can be ruthless. Depending on how much is at stake some of them will go to any lengths to get what they want." He looked at her with narrowed eyes. "Cat, promise me you won't go digging around! We don't know yet if anyone working on the five ranches has been planted here by whoever is trying to force the rancher's hand."

"Okay!" Cat shook her head. "I won't."

"Thank you," Wallace said. "I can't be worrying about you while I'm investigating."

"While you're investigating there's someone I want you to

look into for me," Cat told him. "For some reason, I don't trust him, and I've found him snooping around."

"You should've told me right away!" Wallace said. "What's his name?"

"David Miller," Cat said. "He's Cupids Bow Ranch's foreman."

"David Miller?" Wallace raised one eyebrow. "Name sounds familiar."

Cat frowned. She had a feeling Wallace already knew who David was and something about him. But she wasn't going to push him. Cat had realized a while ago that Wallace had his own way of working. At first, it had worried her, but she'd soon realized that everything he did was to ensure her safety.

"I'd better get back to Zac," Cat said. "Would you mind helping Maria with Magenta when she arrives? You know how temperamental my horse can be."

"I will," Wallace promised. "Are you going to be okay here on your own?"

"I'm not on my own, I have Zac and all the people on the ranch around me," Cat assured him.

"I'll walk you back to Zac's house and make sure our watcher, as well as our tail, have gone," Wallace said.

"Okay," Cat didn't mind him walking her back to the house.

Cat was feeling a little creeped out that Wallace thought someone had been watching them and another person tailing them.

Cat walked into Zac's house after saying goodbye to Wallace, and was immediately greeted by David.

"I see Craig gave you a tour of the stables." David smiled.

"Yes, I can't believe what Zac had done with them." Cat's heart was racing as her eyes and David's met and locked.

"Zac wants to expand his horse breeding program," David told her.

"Craig mentioned that," Cat said, walking towards the kitchen to put the kettle on for some coffee.

David followed her and stood on the other side of the kitchen counter, watching her. He was making her nervous, and Cat had to force her hand not to shake while she filled the kettle.

"What do you think of Zac's horses?" David asked her.

"They're beautiful," Cat smiled, hoping it didn't look like a forced smile. "Especially Monarch."

"He's a bit sick right now," David told her. "Zac and the other local vet have been treating him."

"I didn't know Zac still practices as a vet," Cat said, going to the cupboard to get some cups out. "Would you like some coffee or tea?"

"No, thanks," David declined. "I wanted to ask you if you'd like to ride with me tomorrow?"

Cat looked at him, surprised. The fluttering things in her stomach came awake to do a dance, and her heart once again picked up speed. Cat gripped the mugs she was holding to steady her hands before she dropped the cups.

"Where to?" Cat asked him, feeling her throat go dry when her eyes once again locked with his and the dance tempo of the fluttering things inside her belly increased.

"I have to go ride over the south end of the ranch to check the fences that have just been mended," David told her. "I know you said you wanted to divide the ranch into sections to see it. As I have to go there tomorrow, I thought you'd like to start with that section?"

"I'm sure if all is well with Magenta, she'd need a good ride by tomorrow." Cat dragged her eyes away from him and busied herself making the coffee. "What time?"

Cat put the cups on a tray and got some of the cookies Zac liked to put on a plate.

"Is seven in the morning too early for you?" David grinned when she gave him a scathing look.

"I'm still a country girl at heart, David," Cat said indignantly.

"I may have moved to the city but I'm still ninety-six percent country, and as such my country clock still works."

"I take it that you mean you'll be up and ready by then?" David laughed and winked at her.

"I know you're trying to make me think you're only teasing me," Cat said. "But I have a suspicion that you don't believe me."

"I am teasing you," David assured her. He glanced at his wristwatch. "I have to go and supervise some work on the ranch. I'll see you at the Cupids Bow stables bright and early tomorrow."

"I'll be there," Cat assured him.

"I'm also looking forward to showing you some of the trails along the way," David told her before walking off.

Cat stood staring at the front door after David walked out of it. She was trying to get a grip on the excitement that had curled through her when David said he was looking forward to their ride.

"What is wrong with you, Cat?" Cat said to herself softly. "It's not a social ride. It's for business."

But saying it out loud made no difference to the crazy, excited, fluttering things in her belly. As much as she tried to deny it to herself, Cat was also looking forward to going for a ride with David tomorrow.

Cat had ridden every day she could over the past thirty-one years she'd been away from Montana. Although she'd enjoyed every single ride, there was nothing like the feeling of galloping across the wide, open plains of Montana. Cat maneuvered Magenta towards Cupids Bow Ranch. She pulled the quarter horse to a stop as she got near the property gate that separated Big Mountain Ranch from Cupids Bow. Cat reached down and unlatched the gate, making Magenta carefully walk through it before sliding off the horse. She may be able to open the gate on her horse, but closing it was a whole different story. Cat hadn't slept much the previous night because those stupid fluttering things in her stomach had been going wild as she'd thought about today. What the heck was wrong with her?

David Miller was not to be trusted. Every instinct she had was warning her about it. Yet just the thought of the man made her heart skip a beat.

"I'm going to put this down to fascination," Cat mumbled to herself as she closed the property border gate. "It must be some residual leftover emotion from that first day."

She looked up at Magenta who was standing patiently, waiting for her.

"What do you think, girl?" Cat rubbed the horse's forehead.

"You know, talking to a horse is still classed as talking to yourself," the object of her thoughts' voice came from behind her making her jump.

Cat whirled around so fast to look up at David on his horse that she nearly lost her Stetson. Her hand flew up to steady it on her head.

"Are you crazy?" Cat hissed at him. "You nearly scared me half to death, again!" She glared at him. "How did you sneak up behind me so quietly on your horse?"

"That's because Clive is as stealthy and silent as a jungle cat." David laughed and slid off his horse. "This must be Magenta."

"Yes, but I wouldn't do..." Before Cat could finish her sentence Magenta surprised Cat. Instead of her usual bite, Magenta gently nose-bumped David's hand. "She usually bites people she doesn't know." Her eyes narrowed at David. "Do you have fruit in your pocket?"

"Uh..." David frowned at her. "I'm wearing jeans and a shirt! Do you see any fruit on me?"

"That's weird," Cat said.

"Maybe she just likes me." David laughed when Magenta nudged him again for some more attention. "They say horses are good judges of character," he teased Cat.

"Sure, they are," Cat muttered, swinging herself back onto

Magenta before David could help her. "Traitor," she whispered to Magenta.

"You're early," David observed, swinging his long frame effortlessly onto his horse.

"I told you, I like to get up early and ride," Cat said, spurring Magenta into a walk. "What are you doing on this side of the property so early?"

"I too like to get up early and go for a ride," David told her, walking Clive next to them. "I also thought I'd come and meet you at the gate so we could head straight out."

"Well then, what are you waiting for?" Cat said and kicked Magenta into a gallop.

David laughed as Cat and Magenta pulled away. "I see that's how you want to play this?"

David and Cat galloped towards the south side of the property, reigning in the horses when they came to the Cupid River crossing that ran through the ranch. The horses were skittish and antsy because of what they found along the banks of the river.

"What the heck?" David swung off the back of Clive, gently settling him down.

"Oh, no." Cat slid off Magenta and lightly tethered her to a tree a few feet away from the scene.

Cat ran towards the young moose struggling to get up. Its mother was lying near him, breathing shallowly and hardly moving.

"Cat, be careful," David warned, trying to quickly tether a very nervous Clive.

"It's okay, girl," Cat cooed slowly walking up to the moose. "David, you need to call the ranch and tell them to get Jamie here now!"

"Cat please be careful; the mother moose may just stand up and try to bolt," David said, pulling out his phone and dialing.

The baby moose was anxiously trying to get up and run, but it was too weak. Cat sat down beside the momma moose and cautiously put a hand near its nostrils. The animal's eyes remained closed, and her breathing was becoming more labored.

"Hang in there, big girl," Cat said soothingly. "Help is on its way. I'm going to check on your baby and I promise you I'm not going to hurt it, but you both need help."

"Jamie and Darren are on their way," David told Cat as he cautiously made his way over to where she was, trying not to startle the baby moose any more than it already was.

David dropped down onto his knees and expertly grabbed the baby moose, turning it onto its side with its legs away from him so he could get to its head. "It looks like it's been poisoned."

"Just what the heck is going on here?" Cat hissed, her eyes narrowing into angry slits. "Is there a plant out here that's doing this to the animals?"

Cat looked around at the foliage around the river banks but there were no plants that she didn't recognize.

"We've been trying to figure that out for a while now," David told her. "However, we thought we'd stopped all this when the Hicks family moved away five years ago."

"Hicks?" Cat frowned. "You know I don't remember any Hicks family near here."

For some reason, Cat held back the fact that Maria had already told her about the Hicks family. There was something in his voice and eyes that made her think he knew the Hicks family a lot better than he was letting on.

"Ron Hicks took over the Donaldson Ranch on the other side of Four Lakes Ranch," David explained, trying to keep the baby moose as calm as he could. "He and his three kids caused a lot of trouble throughout Lewistown."

"Are those the people that put Hayden in the hospital when he was eighteen?" Cat asked David.

"I believe so," David said. "I wasn't here when all that happened."

"Was it the Hicks that were poisoning the cattle?" Cat frowned. "Why would they do that?"

"At first, Zac and the other ranches around here thought that

Ron Hicks had bought the Donaldson Ranch when Old man Donaldson passed away," David grunted as the baby moose tried to pull away once again. "Turns out that Ron Hicks was old man Donaldson's second eldest grandson, the son of his youngest daughter."

"So, you think this is all a vendetta?" Cat's eyes widened. "There's been a feud between all the ranches that border Cupids Bow. That was more anger over some dispute that happened generations ago." She jumped back when the momma moose's body jolted.

"They've definitely been poisoned." David's voice was laced with genuine anger. "Zac told me about the feud between the five ranches. But now it's more of a cold shoulder than anything else."

"Yes," Cat nodded. "My generation decided it was time to put whatever differences we had aside. We all grew up together and went to school together. We were actually friends." She shook her head. "Then, when we became young adults, something changed. But still, there was no bad blood. But between the five ranches and the Donaldson family, there's a lot of bad blood."

"Do you know why?" David asked her.

There was something in his voice that made Cat know he already knew her answer. She frowned at him, "No," Cat shook her head. "Do you?" Her eyes narrowed as she watched him intently when he answered.

"Not all of it," David told her, getting into a more comfortable position, and pulling the baby moose's head onto his lap. "It has something to do with land rights."

"Oh?" Cat's brow furrowed even more. She knew he was trying to bait her, but she wasn't biting. "They're poisoning our animals, including the wildlife, over a land dispute?"

"It seems that way," David told her. "You don't realize what people will do for land or money. And when it comes right down to it, the two are actually the same thing. Cupids Bow and the other four ranches that border it are on prime land."

"Land that has been in all the families of those ranches for generations," Cat pointed out. "Long before the Donaldsons settled here."

"According to Ron Hicks, the Donaldsons were short sold on the land they bought," David explained. "They think they are entitled to the few acres that were paid for and never given over to them."

"Which acres would those be?" Cat asked him. "Are they talking about the forest channel that runs around his property into the mountains?"

David shrugged instead of answering her directly, making Cat think he was hiding something. "That land actually belongs to Cupids Bow. But my grandfather a few generations removed deemed it a neutral alley that all five ranches could use. The Donaldson ranch also belonged to Cupids Bow once."

"I'm sure that there are leases or deeds somewhere," Cat said. "Surely, they would rather get things done legally? Poisoning the animals and causing trouble for the ranches seems a bit extreme over a fight for land."

"Like I said," David looked at her, "land equates to money, and people do anything for it."

"Yes, but it still doesn't make sense that the Hicks family would go to such extremes for that land," Cat pointed out again. "You can't do anything with it because of the forest."

"I told you what I know." David moved a little, obviously getting uncomfortable. "Stay still, little fellow." He shook his head. "Do you think you could help me keep him still? The more he moves about the more harm it's causing to itself."

"Okay," Cat carefully moved towards where David was sitting.

"If you can gently hold the back of him still," David inclined his head. "That will stop him from trying to kick out."

Cat nodded and gently held the baby moose's back legs down by leaning across its body. "He's quite prickly."

"Yes, that's the guard hairs," David said. "Their undercoat is quite soft."

Before Cat could answer, the sound of an approaching vehicle caught their attention. It was Zac's vet practice jeep. Jamie was driving it. She pulled to a stop near the horses and jumped out of the vehicle. Her passenger was a handsome young man who, if Cat had to guess, was about Jamie's age. The two of them rushed over to where David and Cat were sitting, trying to keep the very stressed out baby moose still.

"Hi, Aunt Cat," Jamie greeted her. "Hi, David." She looked back at the young man. "This is Darren. He's the new vet dad hired."

"Hi," Cat greeted Darren, who returned her greeting.

"Darren and I will take it from here," Jamie told Cat. "Darren, will you swap places with my aunt? She can help me prepare the sedative."

"What?" Cat looked at Jamie surprised.

"Dad told me that you used to help Granddad inject the animals," Jamie said, assessing the baby moose. "We need to get him back to the animal hospital quickly."

Jamie stood up and went to the mother whom she examined. Jamie's eyes were shadowed and her face sad when she stood up and shook her head. "We can try to do something for the momma, but I'm afraid it's too late for her."

"No." Cat's heart dropped.

"Don't worry, Jamie will try," Darren assured Cat. "So will I," he promised. "David, can you help me get them both into the back of the jeep once Jamie has sedated them?"

"Of course," David said.

It didn't take Jamie long to sedate the animals. David and Darren worked quickly to get the animals settled at the back of the jeep. It wasn't long until Jamie and Darren were speeding off to the vet hospital, leaving a shaken Cat and an angry David behind.

"This has just gone way too far," David hissed beneath his breath.

When he turned towards Cat, she saw the anger flashing in his eyes.

Chapter Eight

THE SOUTH FIELDS OF CUPIDS BOW RANCH

"Liam said it wasn't the water that was contaminated," Cat said. "If it wasn't the water then what are the animals consuming?"

"Good question," David said. "We've been trying to figure that out. The last time this happened a couple of years ago we tested everything, but it all came back clean."

"By everything do you mean the soil and grass as well?" Cat asked.

"Yes," David nodded. "It all came back negative. A couple of months after Hayden was hurt by the Hicks boys, Ryan Beckett, from Four Lakes Ranch, found some dead calves."

Cat swung up onto Magenta while David mounted Clive.

"Had they been poisoned?" Cat spurred Magenta into a walk as they headed for the bridge that stretched over the river.

"Yes," David said. "The grass near where the calves had been grazing was turning a weird shade of brown." He shook his head. "The grass area was found to have a form of cyanide in it."

"Oh, my word," Cat looked at him wide-eyed.

They crossed over the river to the other side and carried on walking the horses while they spoke.

"It took months before they could use that pasture again," David told her. "The same thing happened to Cupids Bow

Ranch, and then Double A ranch. The last ranch to be hit was the worst, Mountain Rise Ranch."

"Are they sure it wasn't that ex-Cupids Bow Foreman that my ex-sister-in-law Chelsea was having an affair with?" Cat said, not meaning for it to sound as spiteful as it did.

"Chelsea never had an affair, Cat," David put her straight. "And no, it wasn't Harris Conway who was responsible for the poisonings."

"How could they be so sure?" Cat said. "Did they find out who it was?"

"They suspected it to be the work of Ron Hicks and his sons," David told her. "Ron was a small shareholder in a development company that his grandfather started."

"Old man Donaldson?' Cat frowned.

"Yes." David nodded. "Old man Donaldson's oldest grandson took over the business from him a few years after he bought the land that is now the Donaldson Ranch."

"He had more grandchildren?" Cat asked. "Like I said, I never even knew he had children; he was quite the recluse. The only people who really knew him were his ranch hands and other household staff members."

"He had three daughters and a son," David told her. "His son was the oldest and had a twin sister. They were both killed in a car crash when they were in their twenties."

Cat looked up at David when she heard a catch in his voice. A shadow flitted across his eyes but was gone too fast for Cat to decipher it. Once again, she got that feeling David was hiding something and had to stop herself from shuddering when a chill crept up her spine.

"That's horrible," Cat breathed. "I hope they didn't have any children?"

"I believe the daughter that was killed had a son," David told her. "He was the one who took over old man Donaldson's development company. He took it from a small, very lucrative firm to a massive global company."

"You know an awful lot about the Donaldsons." Cat's eyes narrowed when she looked at him.

"Know the enemy," David said. "Did Zac tell you why I took over as foreman of Cupids Bow Ranch?"

"No," Cat shook her head. "Zac never mentioned you to me once. The first I'd heard that you were the foreman of Cupids Bow was when you fetched me from Billings Airport.

"Ah," David nodded. "Well, the last foreman, the one after Harris, was a drunk with a bad gambling habit. He was easily swayed by a few bucks, which he'd basically do anything for."

"Let me guess, because he had easy access to Cupids Bow and the other four ranches, he was Ron Hicks' informant?" Cat guessed.

"Something like that," David confirmed. "It was also him that was using cyanide to poison the livestock."

"Did he flip on Hicks?" Cat looked at David. Once again, their eyes locked for a few seconds and tiny electric shocks zinged through her body.

"Yes," David nodded. "But when they went to arrest Ron and his family, they were gone."

"Didn't you say he'd sold the ranch?" Cat asked him.

"He did," David told her. "To his other cousin who was part-owner of the ranch. I was looking for something to do at the time they arrested the previous foreman. My father had recently retired, and we sold off our ranch near Billings. I knew horses and how to work the land, so Zac offered me the job."

"Oh, is that all?" Cat looked at him feeling disappointed. The way he'd spoken about how he'd got the job had made her think there was an exciting story behind it. "I thought there was some heroic tale behind Zac offering you the job."

"There was," David told her with a smile. "I know Ron Hicks and I was able to give Zac information that led to his arrest. He's been in prison for the past fifteen years, so I doubt this new bout of poisoning has anything to do with him."

"You said Ron Hicks had three children," Cat pointed out.

"Any one of them could be doing this. Especially if they still have access to the Donaldson ranch if their uncle owns it."

"I don't think their uncle associates with the Hicks side of the family," David said, almost like he had firsthand knowledge of that fact. "He is too much of a businessman to do anything as stupid as to poison land, water, or cattle to get land to develop."

Cat's head shot back around to look at David once again. "Did you say develop?" Her eyes narrowed. "I thought someone trying to develop this land was ruled out as to why this was happening?"

"It's not uncommon for unscrupulous developers to try and starve people who won't sell off their land and then buy it at a reduced rate when it's seized and auctioned off." David scanned the land ahead of them. "But there are also development companies that like to keep things above board."

"That's about the third or fourth time you've defended Donaldson's development company," Cat pointed out.

"I don't recall defending them at all," David told her. "I've been pointing out that there are good and bad sides to everything in life. One cousin might be a troll while the other a decent guy, trying to do the right thing and set things right."

"David, do you know the owner of Donaldson's development company?" Cat looked at him intently, waiting to see how he answered.

"Anyone who's into construction or large scale developments knows him," was all David said. "I dabbled in development and construction for a while."

"You seem to be a Jack of all trades." Cat laughed, trying to keep her unease from her voice. She was now more convinced than ever that David was lying to her about how he knew the Donaldsons.

"It took me a while to find my place in the world," David told her. "But I think I finally have because I've been the foreman of Cupids Bow Ranch for the past fifteen years."

"So, you want to be a ranch foreman for the rest of your life?" Cat looked at him questioningly.

"No," David shook his head. "I've been trying to convince Zac to let me become a partner in his horse breeding program."

"How are you planning to do that?" Cat pulled Magenta to a stop, and David reigned Clive in. "Sorry, I just need some water." She reached over to her saddlebags. "Would you like one?"

"Please," David nodded and took the bottle of water Cat handed him. "To answer your previous question, I can raise the capital to invest in the breeding program and expand it to where Zac wants it to be."

"How are you able to raise the amount of money I can only imagine a venture like that would cost?" Cat opened her bottle of water and took a long swallow.

"I got a share of my father's ranch when he sold it," David told her. "I invested that money to save for a rainy day."

"Okay," Cat was impressed. "You do know that having a stake in the horse breeding program doesn't mean you have any claim to Cupids Bow Ranch?"

"I do," David nodded. "I don't want a claim on the ranch. I want a claim in the horse breeding program. Zac and I can get some excellent horse breeds. I even know someone with a Percheron that will be old enough to breed around the time Pegasus would be."

"Have you spoken to Zac about this already?" Cat took one last swallow of her water before putting the bottle back in her saddlebag."

"Yes," David told her and finished his water. He put his empty bottle in his saddlebag too. "We're in negotiations over it."

"Keep me posted on the outcome," Cat said. "Should we carry on?" She spurred Magenta into a trot.

David caught up with them and they continued their journey towards the south fields. Along the way, David showed Cat some of the trails he and Zac had developed for their guests at the inn. He explained Zac's plans to try and introduce summer mountain hikes. Zac also wanted to start offering skiing packages where he'd take his exclusive guests to Showdown ski resort for day trips during skiing season.

By the time they'd come to the south side of the ranch, after all their detours, and stops along the way, it was already late morning. Cat was starving as she hadn't had breakfast. David had brought some sandwiches and snacks the kitchen at Cupids Bow Inn had packed for them. Cat hadn't been shy about wolfing down two of the delicious sandwiches. They were made from home-baked bread and freshly churned butter, a taste that Cat had longed for all the years she'd been away from home.

"Bessie used to bake this exact bread," Cat said, finishing off her last sandwich.

"It's Bessie's recipe," David told her. "She left it for Janine to use at the inn when she retired."

"I believe she moved to Florida?" Cat said, drinking some more water.

"Yes," David nodded. "She's remarried now. Bessie and her new husband come here from time to time on vacation, but they're mostly having fun sailing around the world."

"I'm glad for Bessie." Cat sighed and leaned back. They were sitting on a picnic blanket David had brought with him.

"Me too. And for my father." David grinned.

"Bessie married your father?" Cat's eyes widened.

"She did," David confirmed. "My father's previous wife had passed away five years before they met. Her husband had been gone for three. They both clicked the moment I introduced them."

"Oh, so you're the reason Cupids Bow lost their best housekeeper?" Cat teased him. "I have met your father, but I only knew him as Joe."

"That's my dad," David said proudly. "He's a good man that's been through a lot in his life." He finished another bottle of water.

"His previous wife?" Cat frowned. "You mean your mother?"

"No," David shook his head. "My mother died when I was a month away from turning one. I didn't know her. But Jackie raised me like I was her own son because she couldn't have children of her own."

"Jackie was your father's previous wife?" Cat guessed.

"That's right." David nodded. "They were together for a long time. My father was devastated when he lost her. He couldn't believe that he'd lost another wife."

"Oh, your poor dad." Cat's heart broke for Joe.

Cat had only met Joe twice when Bessie had come to Nashville to see two of her concerts. Bessie and Joe had stayed with her in her Nashville apartment and her Brentwood home on both occasions.

"His first wife left him with a five-month-old son," David explained. "He married my mother six months later, and then two years later she passed away. It took him a while to get over my mother's death, but then he met Jackie and now he has Bessie."

"Wow!" Cat said. "That's quite a family history you have there" She frowned as something he said sank in. "You have an older brother?"

"I do," David nodded. "But we haven't spoken to each other in many years."

"That's sad," Cat started to pack up their late breakfast.

"You didn't come home for many years," David pointed out, helping her.

She stood up so he could roll up the blanket, "But I still kept in touch with Bessie and my brother."

"You mean you kept up with Zac via Bessie," David reminded her. "Zac was really worried about you when you left."

"What? Did he go crying on your shoulder?" Cat shook her head.

"You didn't even go to his wedding." David packed the breakfast items back into his saddlebags and hooked the blanket in place.

"I couldn't make it," Cat told him, putting her hat back on her head. "Did you go to your brother's wedding?"

"How do you know he was even married?" David looked at her.

"Assumption," Cat shrugged.

"I did," David nodded. "Both of them."

"He was married twice?" Cat closed her saddlebags.

"Are you judging?" David teased her to lighten the mood Cat guessed.

"Nope." Cat shook her head. "Just asking."

"He was," David told her. "His first wife died in action. They were in the military together. His second wife was more interested in our father's money than she was in him."

"Oh, gosh." Cat felt awful for bringing it up. "Your family has quite the marriage track record."

"It does." David waited for Cat to swing onto Magenta before climbing onto his horse.

"What about you?" Cat had no idea why the question had popped out of her mouth. Then her eyes immediately went to his ring finger.

"I was married," David admitted, turning Clive in the direction he needed to go.

Cat and Magenta followed them. She couldn't stop herself from asking, "What happened?"

"She left me for my no-good cousin," David shrugged. "Our marriage was about over before she decided to run off with him. The only good thing she did was leave our four year old daughter, Waverly, with me."

"You have a daughter?" Cat looked at him surprised.

"Why do you look so surprised that I have a child?" David frowned.

"I just can't picture you as the family type," Cat told him honestly.

"How do you picture me?" David's eyes locked with hers.

Cat's heart started to pound, and the annoying fluttering made her breath catch in her throat. "I... um..." She cleared her throat and dragged her eyes away from his hypnotic gaze, hoping to calm her traitorous emotions. "Just like a bachelor." She said the first thing she could think of.

"Oh, thank you," David said, sarcastically, pulling Clive to a stop. "So, what you really mean by that is a playboy scoundrel type?"

"That's not what I said," Cat told him, stopping beside them.

They were at one of the fence lines and she heard David draw in an angry breath as he said, "What the blazers?"

Cat looked in the direction he was looking. One of the fences was down and looked as if it had been cut. "Does that look like it's been cut?"

She looked at David, who turned towards her. His eyes were flashing with anger but then widened as something near her shoulder caught his attention. But before she could look down to see what it was, he grabbed her and pulled her from her horse. David lost his balance and they tumbled to the ground as a loud crack split the air. The horses reared, turned, and started to run off when another crack resounded. David grabbed Cat and rolled her over as something zinged passed her cheek just nicking it, making it sting.

"What the ..." Cat wheezed, then all the breath whooshed out of her when David dropped down over her, covering her, as yet another blast disrupted the quiet.

"We need to move," David breathed.

Cat was winded, her cheek stung, and her brain felt foggy with confusion. *What had just happened?* David rolled off her.

"Cat," David looked at her and rolled onto his stomach, "follow me."

Cat nodded. Her mind reeled as she realized that what they'd heard had been gunshots that had been aimed at her. Before she could give in to the fear threatening to paralyze her, Cat found the strength to follow David's lead and leopard-crawled behind a large bush.

"Were those gunshots?" Cat's chest rose and fell, her heart was no longer pounding from being close to David but from the adrenaline activating her fight or flight response. "How did you know to pull me off my horse?"

Cat's suspicion of David became intensified by her heightened senses.

"There was a red dot on your shirt," David winced when he touched his shoulder.

"You could've killed us both pulling us from our horses like that," Cat hissed at him.

The shock she'd just had started to resound through her.

"A few broken bones are a lot better than a bullet to the heart," Zac pulled his hand away from his shoulder and Cat's eyes widened when she saw the blood.

"Were you hit?" Cat asked. Without thinking, she leaned over him and pulled the side of his cotton shirt down. "You've been hit."

There was a long gash on the side of his arm.

"It's just a scratch," David assured her. "The same bullet that nicked your face got me."

Cat's hand immediately went to the side of her face. She'd been so scared and determined to get to safety that she'd forgotten about the stinging on the side of her face.

"Is it deep?" Cat asked him, turning her face so he could see.

"You may need a few stitches," David told her. "But right now, we need to find the horses and get the heck away from here."

"Do you think whoever shot at us will come looking for us to finish the job?" Cat started to feel the fear and panic rise inside her.

"I think we don't want to find out," David told her calmly. "Just stay close to me and do what I say."

"Okay." Cat nodded.

"The horses took off in that direction, into the trees." David pointed toward the tree line behind them. "Are you ready to make a run for it?"

"I think so?" Cat said, ignoring the pain in her ribs.

David stood up, but kept low within the bush line, he reached for Cat's hand, who crouched next to him.

"Ready?" David looked at her and she nodded.

He stood and before she knew what was happening David scooped her up into his arms. He dashed towards the tree line. As they made it into the tree covering, David dashed to the right as another shot rang through the air.

"He's moving in," David warned her. "Hang on."

Cat wasn't arguing with him. She wrapped her arms around him and cushioned her head against his solid, broad chest.

"We need to call for help," David said, sounding out of breath as he zig-zagged through the trees, getting deeper and deeper into the forest. "Can you reach into my back pocket and get my phone?

Cat nodded, "Which side?"

"The right," David told her.

Cat reached her hand around his back and found the phone. She pulled it from his pocket. "Got it," she told him.

"Okay," David huffed. "I'm going to get up behind that rock covering up ahead."

He took the final steps and ducked down behind the wall of rocks. David gently lowered Cat to the ground before plopping down next to her and leaning against the wall.

"What is your passcode?" Cat asked him.

David gave it to her while he sat, getting his breath back. "Look for Ryan Beckett's number. He's the closest to us and I know he's working the fields close by."

"What if it's him that's shooting at us?" Cat said.

"Trust me, it's not Ryan," David assured her.

"How can you be so sure?" Cat asked him, scrolling through his phone until she found Ryan's number.

"Because Ryan wouldn't have missed a shot like that," David told her.

"Oh, that makes me feel so much better about phoning him." Cat shook her head as she dialed the number.

"Cat?" Ryan answered almost immediately. "Where are you and David?"

"Uh..." Cat's eyes grew wide with alarm. She put the phone against her as she looked at David. "I think it is Ryan who's trying to kill us."

"I'm not the one shooting at you!" Ryan called through the phone.

"Of course, you're going to say that." Cat put the phone back against her ear.

"Oh, good grief," Ryan hissed. "Put David on the phone, please, Cat."

"He wants to talk to you." Cat handed David the phone.

Before David could say anything, another shot resounded through the air.

"I've got to go, stay wherever you both are," Ryan warned, and then hung up.

"How many darn bullets are in that rifle?" Cat jumped when another shot was fired. "Is it just me or did that shot sound a lot closer?"

"Nope, it wasn't just you," David said. "Stay down!" He warned her and carefully turned to peak around the rock. He quickly sat back against the rock. "Don't make a sound." His voice dropped to a whisper.

Cat nodded and instinctively moved closer to hide beside David's large form. Everything went deathly quiet for what felt like an eternity, but Cat knew it was only a few seconds before they heard footsteps and a snap of a twig. Her heart felt like it had stopped, and her breath caught in her throat as she kept as quiet as she could. Cat was even too scared to breathe.

David's large warm hand closed over hers and he drew her closer beside him as they huddled down behind the rock wall. Everything went deathly silent once again and they sat there waiting. Then they heard a familiar voice.

"Don't move!" Cat heard Ryan Beckett say. "Put the rifle down then lace your fingers together behind your head." There was a pause. "Now on your knees."

Cat and David didn't move.

"Hi, I found him," Ryan said to someone, and Cat presumed he was on his phone. "I don't know where they are but once you've picked this guy up, I'll go find them. Have you found their horses?"

Another pause. "Good, I'll let you know once I've found them. I'm not sure if they're hurt."

"I told you it wasn't Ryan who was shooting at us," David whispered.

"He could be pretending," Cat pointed out.

"You really have trust issues, don't you?" David shook his head.

Cat noticed that even though David knew Ryan had their shooter subdued, he hadn't let go of her hand or moved away from her. Then again neither had she, and that's when she made herself admit that she had conflicting emotions about David. He'd fascinated her when she was eighteen and intrigued her by his mysterious vanishing act. She'd be lying if she said she hadn't wondered about David over the years. Cat even had to stop herself on numerous occasions from trying to look him up on social media.

Chapter Nine

PEGASUS THE WARRIOR

David felt the adrenaline pumping through his veins, but he knew it wasn't just because of the action he and Cat had been through. The moment he laid eyes on Cat again when he went to fetch her at the Billings airport, David had known he still had feelings for her. Although he would never admit it to himself, deep down David had always known that every woman he'd met after Cat was an emotional filler. That's why he could never blame or be angry at his ex-wife when she'd had enough and walked out on him. What he could never forgive his ex-wife for was completely abandoning their daughter.

But he'd soon found out that he and Waverly didn't need anyone else in their lives. David and his daughter had a very good father-daughter relationship. She was currently working her way into the supreme court justice system and David couldn't be prouder. Waverly had big dreams and set goals that she didn't let anything make her waver from. She reminded him of his older brother in that way.

"Do you think it's safe to let Ryan know where we are now?" Cat whispered. "Or are you now having doubts about Ryan as well?"

Cat's voice broke through his thoughts.

"I don't have doubts about Ryan," David assured her. "What

I'm worried about is whether whoever was shooting us was alone or not."

"Thank you for that thought," Cat said. "I may never move from this spot now."

"Don't worry, Ryan will call for us when he's sure we're safe," David said. "We've just got to sit tight until he does."

"Okay," Cat whispered.

David noticed her rubbing her temple on the side, where the bullet nicked her beautiful face. "Are you getting a headache?" He looked at her worriedly, wondering if she'd hit her head at all.

"It's nothing," Cat told him. "I think it's all the excitement from being yanked from my horse."

"You are never going to let that go, are you?" David shook his head.

"At least not anytime soon," Cat said. "How's your arm?"

"I'll live." David shrugged.

He heard movement and put his finger to his lips indicating for Cat to be quiet. She nodded. Then the breath caught in his throat when she put her head on his shoulder.

"I've checked both properties and there are no signs he had an accomplice," another male voice said. "The police are on their way and will arrive with the chopper in a few minutes."

"Thank you," David heard Ryan say. "I'll go look for Cat and David. Keep an eye on him and don't let him move a muscle."

"Will do, boss," the man said.

"Cat, David," Ryan's voice drifted to them. "You can come out now, we have the shooter."

"Do you think we can believe him?" Cat whispered.

David wanted to say no because he didn't want to move away from her, but he knew they both needed medical attention and to find their horses. He took a breath and nodded.

"Yes, we can believe him." David smiled at her, holding onto her hand for a few seconds longer, savoring the feeling of it cupped in his. "Ready?"

"I guess," Cat said. "But I'm warning you now if Ryan turns out to be the bad guy, this is on you!"

"Fair enough," David agreed with a soft laugh before reluctantly letting go of her hand and standing up.

But as he did, a searing hot pain ripped through his shoulder. His head immediately turned towards Cat and before he could think he grabbed her once again, pulling her to the ground.

"I told you!" Cat hissed at him.

"Are you two alright?" Ryan appeared next to them and ducked behind the rock.

"Get away from us, you murderer." Cat flew at Ryan, her tiny fists flying.

"Cat, no." David grabbed her, ignoring the pain reverberating through his arm.

"Nice to see you too, Kitty Cat," Ryan said.

"What the heck, Ryan?" David glared at him. "I thought your man said there wasn't anyone else?"

"Turns out he was the other man," Ryan told David calmly. "Not to worry though, I did have my suspicions about him."

"What the heck?" a male voice screamed from the other side of the rock.

There was a loud whinny and more male shouting right before the sound of a helicopter and police sirens were heard. Ryan, David, and Cat carefully lifted their heads above the rock and were shocked by the sight they saw.

"Oh, my word!" Cat's eyes were huge.

"Is that ..." Ryan looked at David and then Cat in astonishment.

"Pegasus," David told them, shaking his head. "Craig told me the horse was besotted with Cat and he had to put him in his stable because he was trying to follow you yesterday."

"Did he really just come to save us?" Cat pointed at the huge horse. "How did he even know where we were?"

"He must've followed us," David guessed.

"No way," Cat breathed.

Soon the police had descended on the scene. Ryan called out to them and put the rifle he had in hand down before stepping out from behind the rock.

"Hey, Gerry," Ryan called to the police captain who'd arrived on the scene. "Thanks for the quick response."

"Is anyone hurt?" Gerry asked Ryan.

"Yes," Ryan nodded. "David Miller has been shot through the shoulder and needs medical attention. So does Cat Sparrow, but hers is not as urgent."

"Thanks, Ryan," Cat hissed as she stood up and smiled at Gerry. "Hi, Gerry." She waved at her old school friend.

"Cat?" Gerry grinned. "It's good to see you. I just wish it was under different circumstances."

"Are there any medics?" Cat asked Gerry. "David needs urgent attention."

"They're right behind me," Gerry assured her, cuffing the two men.

"Hold still, Pegasus." Cat tilted her head when she heard Jamie's voice. "Jamie?"

"Hi, Aunt Cat." Jamie glanced at her. "I was trying to find this brute who ran off after I returned to the ranch after I was finished with attending to the moose."

"He came looking for you," David told her. "I'm just going to sit down for a second."

David's arm was on fire, and he was feeling light-headed. He gripped the rock in front of him to steady himself.

"David, are you okay?" Jamie managed to get the halter on Pegasus' face along with the lead rope. She rushed towards where they were standing. "Can you hold him, please?" She handed the lead to Ryan.

"You know this horse and I don't get along," Ryan told her.

"What was that you told me when I fell off my horse that time at the rodeo?" Jamie asked him. "Don't let him control you, you control him, show him who's boss." She gave him a smug smile.

"Fine." Ryan shook his head and took the lead rope. "Come on, brute."

But Pegasus would not move. He stood staring at Ryan as if daring him to try and move him.

"Have fun," Jamie patted Ryan on the shoulder and stepped up next to David. "Sit!" she commanded.

"Thanks, kid," Ryan glared at her. "I don't think he's going to go anywhere until he's ready to."

"Just see to it that he doesn't run away," Jamie said.

"I'm not a dog," David grumbled and carefully sat down.

"Then don't make me treat you like one," Jamie warned him. "I do have some animal tranquilizers in my jeep."

"Thanks, but I'll pass," David told her. "Aren't you a vet?"

"Until the medics get here, I'm all that you've got," Jamie pointed out. "And that bullet wound needs attention right now."

Jamie pulled her soft cotton shirt off and crumpled it into a ball. "Aunt Cat, could you please hold this against David's arm?"

"Sure," Cat said and knelt next to Jamie.

"I'm going to get some medical supplies in the jeep and find out where that chopper Captain Gerry said was right behind him is," Jamie told them. "I'll be right back."

"I'm sorry that your first ride along turned into a nightmare," David told Cat.

"It's not your fault," Cat said. "I think whoever that man is, he's been following me for a while now."

"You should've told me or Zac that you were being stalked." David's protective instincts immediately kicked in. "Cat, what if you were alone when he struck?"

"I only found out yesterday that someone was watching and following me," Cat told him. "I haven't had time since then to tell anyone. Besides, my bodyguard knows, and is looking into it."

"You have a bodyguard now, Cat?" Ryan popped his head over the rock wall. "Why wasn't he with you today?"

"Because I needed him to be somewhere else," was all Cat told Ryan.

David frowned, wondering where that somewhere else was. What was Cat up to? Better yet, what was her bodyguard up to? David was getting more worried every minute Cat's bodyguard was snooping around. The man could unravel years of hard work and careful planning.

"Cat, you need him to be with you around the clock," Ryan said. "I don't know if you've heard or not, but our ranches have been under an attack once again."

"I did hear," Cat said, looking up at Ryan. "I'm sorry about all the livestock you've lost, Ryan."

"Four Lakes has been luckier than Mountain Rise and Double A," Ryan told her. "They were hit the hardest and were struggling before the trouble started."

"Oh, no!" Cat breathed. "How badly were they affected?"

"Chelsea is struggling the most, Cat," Ryan's voice dropped. "Her mother is not well, and Chelsea is basically hanging on by a thread."

"I didn't know her mother was ill." Cat looked up at Ryan. She put a bit too much pressure on David's wound and he grunted. "I'm sorry, I'm sorry!"

"It's fine," David lied. He felt as if she'd dug a knife into the wound.

"I'm back," Jamie said, rushing to his side. "The medics have been delayed. So, it looks like I really am your only hope right now."

"Great!" David breathed.

"You can let go now," Jamie told Cat. "Why don't you go help Ryan with your number one fan?" She smiled at Cat. "I'm sure you're not going to want to watch me fish a bullet from David's arm."

"I thought it went right through?" David frowned.

"Nope," Jamie filled the syringe with a clear liquid and patted it. "It did not."

"What's in there?" David looked at her feeling a little worried. "Have you ever done this to a human before?"

"I've done it to a horse!" Jamie grinned. "How different could it be?"

"You know, I think I'll wait for the medics," David said.

"Relax," Jamie's voice became more serious. "I promise I know what I'm doing."

"Okay." David's eyes narrowed.

"This is a mild sedative," Jamie told him and, before he knew what was happening, he started to feel relaxed and the pain in his shoulder subsided.

"You've given me the injection already?" David looked at her amazed.

"Uh-huh," Jamie nodded.

"I didn't even feel it," David told her.

"Trust me, after being bitten by an animal a few times, you quickly learn how to give injections as painlessly as possible." Jamie fished in her bag. "I'll give it a few minutes to numb while I clean it."

"Maybe you should teach doctors how to give injections." David's eyelids were feeling incredibly heavy and, eventually, he lost the fight trying to keep them open. He drifted off.

It had been a long morning. Cat was still shaken by the events of it and amazed that Pegasus had tracked her down and then basically saved three lives with his heroics. Horses were truly amazing creatures. After David had passed out the medic helicopter had arrived. David and Cat had been loaded into it, then taken to the hospital. Cat only needed a few butterfly bandages on the wound, her face, and bandaged up bruised ribs. But David had to undergo surgery. Jamie had found that the first bullet had in fact gone into David's arm. He was having two bullets removed and had one cracked rib from breaking Cat's fall from the horse.

Cat was feeling awful that David had saved her life while she'd had Wallace investigate him because she didn't trust him. The man had taken two bullets because of her. Cat was waiting to hear from the police who the man trying to shoot them was and why. She was convinced the man must've been one of

Marshall Myers' crazed fans that hated her, which meant if he had found her, others wouldn't be too far behind. Now that Cat had finally come home to Montana she wanted to stay for a while. But if she was going to get mobbed by angry fans, she really couldn't bring that trouble to the ranches. They already had enough going on without her troubles bubbling over onto them as well.

Cat needed to talk to Wallace.

"Sorry, doctor, can I go?" Cat asked the doctor who was attending to her.

"If you're sure you're feeling okay," the doctor said.

"I'm fine," Cat assured him. "Do you have any news on David Miller, who was brought in with me?"

"He's still in surgery," the doctor told her.

"Thank you." Cat signed the forms the nurse handed her before leaving the room.

When Cat got to the waiting area, she was greeted by Indy, Hayden, Jamie, Maria, and Wallace.

"Mom," Indy pulled her in for a hug, "we were so worried about you." He looked at Cat. "What happened out there?"

Cat greeted the rest of the group waiting for her.

"David and I were riding the south fields. We stopped to examine where a fence had been cut. The next thing I knew I was being pulled off my horse by David as a gunshot resounded through the air."

"Oh, mom." Indy's eyes were filled with concern. "Jamie tells me they have the men in custody and that one of them was a ranch hand of Ryan Becketts." He looked at her with a frown. "You don't think Ryan was involved in the shooting, do you?"

"No, he was as surprised as anyone that his ranch hand was mixed up with the man who shot at us," Cat told them.

"You've had quite an ordeal, Aunt Cat." Hayden shook his head. "We're all glad that you're okay."

"That horse of yours, Jamie is something else," Cat said.

"He's quite the character alright," Jamie sighed. "Unfortunately, he's also a powerful jumper, so he clears a fence effortlessly when he wants to. It's hard to keep him in one place at times."

"Today, I'm grateful for that." Cat suppressed a shudder thinking of what would've happened if Pegasus hadn't come along.

"I'm here to take you back to Big Valley ranch," Maria told her. "Are you ready?"

"What about Zac?" Cat asked, looking at Jamie.

"Don't worry, mom," Indy said. "I'm taking your shift with Uncle Zac today."

"Thank you, sweetheart." Cat kissed his cheek. "I may even lie down. I have a bit of a headache."

"Do you want the doctor to check that out for you?" Maria's eyes widened with concern.

"No." Cat shook her head. "It's nothing that an aspirin and a lie-down can't fix."

Cat and Maria said their goodbyes. Liam promised to call Cat the minute he had news on David.

"So, your date with David didn't end very well, did it?" Maria teased Cat.

Maria pulled the pickup out of the hospital parking lot and turned onto the main road.

"It wasn't a date," Cat pointed out. "No, our ride to inspect the south fields did not end well. All I can say is thank goodness for Ryan Beckett and Pegasus."

"I heard about Ryan and Pegasus." Maria turned off to the side and onto the exit road that would take them towards the ranch. "He's such an amazing horse."

"He is." Cat put her head back against the headrest, closing her eyes. She hadn't been kidding when she said she had a headache. "Are Magenta and Clive, okay?"

"Yes," Maria said. "Magenta is back at Big Valley and in her stable. She's a little edgy but she's fine."

"Thank goodness," Cat breathed a sigh of relief. "I was so worried that one of the horses had been shot."

"No, they're not injured," Maria assured her. "I checked them both out with Jamie."

"You really should've been a vet." Cat turned her head and opened one eye to look at Maria. "You know nearly everything there's to know about animals."

"That's thanks to the after-school summer job I had with the local vet," Maria explained. "Jamie is the truly gifted one when it comes to animals. I'm really glad she became a vet."

"Yes, my niece is wonderful with animals," Cat agreed, closing both her eyes once again.

"Cat, are you sure we don't need to go back to the doctor?" Maria asked her. "You're quite pale."

"I'm fine," Cat assured her again. "Like I said, I need some aspirin and a lie-down."

"I have some aspirin in the glove compartment and there's fresh water in the cooler in the back." Maria gestured to the back of the car with her thumb. "I can pull over and get it for you."

"No," Cat said. "I can get it."

"Why don't you have the aspirin now and get a nap? It's twenty minutes to the ranch," Maria suggested.

"Who's going to keep you company on the journey?" Cat asked, leaning behind the seat and pulling out a bottle of water from the cooler.

"It's not an airplane," Maria pointed out. "I'm fine driving on my own."

"Okay." Cat got the aspirin from the glove compartment and took two out before putting them back.

"My blow-up neck pillow should also be in the glove compartment if you need it," Maria told her.

"No, I'll be fine." Cat took the pills, swallowing them down with some water. "While I'm resting my head, why don't you start telling me everything you know about what's been going on around our ranches over the past years."

"What if you fall asleep?" Maria asked. "Then I'll be sitting here like a crazy person talking to myself."

"I'm not going to go to sleep," Cat told her. "You know I don't like sleeping in a car."

"But you've been injured, so you may just doze off," Maria pointed out.

"Why are you trying to avoid telling me what's been going on around our ranches?" Cat sat up and looked at Maria suspiciously. "You also never told me about Zac turning Cupids Bow into an inn when you knew I never approved that plan."

"I didn't want to worry you," Maria defended her actions. "I thought all the trouble had stopped when they arrested Ron Hicks about fifteen years ago."

"Okay." Cat's eyes narrowed a little more. "I can sort of understand the Ron Hicks thing. But it doesn't explain why you didn't say anything about the inn to me when you've obviously known for a long time."

"Because I was asked not to," Maria told her.

"By Zac?" Cat asked her.

"No," Maria shook her head.

"Who told you not to tell me?" Cat pushed.

"I don't want to get them into trouble," Maria said. "And before you say, 'why would they be in trouble', I know you, Cat. You'll go blazing off on your high horse. Heads will roll and people will cry."

"Good grief, Maria." Cat threw her hand up in exasperation. "You make me sound like a high-spirited filly with a bad attitude."

"That's a great analogy," Maria pointed out with a smile on her face.

"You know what?" Cat dropped back against her seat and closed her eyes. "Don't tell me. I'm leaving as soon as I can anyway. Then I can once again put this all behind me and live in the dark about it like a mushroom."

"What do you mean, you're leaving here soon?" Maria asked her, a little shocked.

"That man who shot at us today," Cat opened her eyes and turned her head, not lifting it from the headrest, "he was aiming for me. David was collateral damage."

"Why do you say that?" Maria's brow was furrowed.

"The reason David was able to pull me off the horse in time was that the shooter was using an infrared scope," Cat told her. "David saw the dot on my shirt."

"What?" Maria's eyes were huge when she looked at Cat. "You're lucky he pulled you off the horse when he did."

"I know." Cat nodded. "I think that man might be one of Marshall's fans. Remember all the hate mail and death threats I've been getting since he told the world what I'd done to him?"

"You think it's a fan?" Maria's eyes widened even more. "Cat, does Wallace know about this?" She glanced at Cat again. "When will West, your manager, arrive?"

"He was supposed to be here already, but he got delayed for some or other reason." Cat shrugged. "Wallace said West was trying to get here by the weekend."

"Cat, I don't think you should leave here," Maria tried to reason with her. "Wait until the police have told you what information they've managed to get from the shooter."

"I intend on waiting around for that information," Cat told her. "But I already know what he's going to say. I can't bring crazed fans down on my family and friends. There's already too much going on at all the ranches."

"Didn't your daddy used to say that regardless of the troubles we're shouldering there's always room to help out your neighbors?" Maria quoted Callum Sparrow.

"My daddy did love his quotes." Cat laughed. "He did say something like that. But this is not the kind of trouble that anyone else can help me shoulder."

"Of course, it is," Maria said hotly. "Weren't you the one who always said not to run from problems or trouble? The Cat Sparrow I know always faces her trouble or problems head-on. She's not even scared of having a head-on collision with them because sometimes the only way is through."

"I was young and naive then," Cat told her. "I thought there was nothing that didn't have a solution to. But I was wrong, and now I know there are some things you have to walk away from." She pinched the bridge of her nose, wishing the aspirin would kick in. "I now know how to pick my fights and when to back off."

"Cat, you and I both know running away is never the answer," Maria said. "Look at us. We both tried and it landed us right back where we started from."

"Yes, but look at what all we achieved because we left," Cat looked on the bright side. "Besides, you know we both couldn't stay here. We had to go."

"Maybe if we'd stayed and sorted things out rather than run, we'd still have achieved great things and your home wouldn't be an inn now," Maria pointed out.

"Yes, but you know that there's no point in should've, what's done is done," Cat said. "We came to a crossroads in our life and chose our paths. Now we just have to hold on tight and hope the road takes us to where we need to be."

"I'm not going to win this, am I?" Maria sighed.

"This isn't a win or lose situation, Maria." Cat turned to look at her. "This is more like a life and death situation. Once again, if I stay, my family and friends could get hurt when they're caught in the crossfire. Or worse, they get used as pawns to get at me."

"You watch too many movies," Maria shook her head. "Let's just wait and see what the police say."

"Okay," Cat agreed. "I've got some investigating to do anyway."

"What are you up to now?" Maria glanced at her again.

Cat leaned back against the seat once again. "I'll tell you if you tell me everything you know about what's going on."

"Deal," Maria said. "I'll make us some cocoa and come up to your room when we're back at Big Valley Ranch. Then we can chat."

"Sounds good." Cat stifled a yawn. "I think I will shut my eyes for the last few minutes of the trip."

Chapter Ten

A SECRET FOR A SECRET

David's head hurt, and his arm, and chest stung. He also felt as if he'd just been hit by a bus. *Maybe he was hit by a bus* was the thought that crossed his mind as he tried to pry his heavy eyelids open.

"What the heck happened to me?" David mumbled to himself trying to force himself to wake up.

"You were shot," a deep familiar voice drawled, giving David a fright.

David wasn't expecting anyone to answer his question. He hadn't even been sure if he'd said it out loud, he was so disorientated. David sighed and flopped back against the hard pillows. *These weren't his pillows*, was the thought that ran through his head.

"No, they are not your pillows because you're in the hospital," the familiar voice told him.

"Are you doing some sort of mind-reading trick?" David was finally able to open his eyes.

Everything was blurred for a few seconds before the world came back into view, and the familiar voice became a familiar face.

"I don't have to mind-read, my hearing is just fine," the person told him. "You've always had that bad habit of mumbling in your sleep and as you're about to wake up. I can't remember the times I've warned you to try and stop doing that."

"We're not all perfect like you, oh superior one," David said sarcastically. "Unlike you, I sleep like a proper person and tend to wake up refreshed. Not looking like I've got bags of sand beneath my eyes."

"Thanks," his visitor said. "I can operate on a couple of hours of sleep a day. But you've never been able to."

Suddenly, images of the day flashed through David's mind and his sleep-fogged thoughts instantly cleared, making him sit up straight in the bed. He immediately regretted the movement, wincing when pain sliced through his chest. That's when he realized that heavy feeling weighing on him was a bandage that wound around his upper torso.

"What the ..." David looked down at his body, trying to pull the covers off, but he regretted that movement as well when pain seared through his upper arm.

"Yeah, you've also got a cracked rib and some badly bruised ones." David's visitor gave him a smug smile.

"Still such a sadist, I see." David looked at his visitor in disgust.

"No, it's payback," his visitor told him.

"Is this still about me shooting out your bike's tire when I was practicing to be a sharpshooter?" David asked, carefully pulling himself into a more comfortable position.

"You could've killed me," his visitor hissed.

"Not likely," David said. "I've always been an excellent shot."

"Tell that to my ankle that you hit," David's visitor reminded him.

"That was a ricocheted, not my fault," David pointed out. "Are you going to tell me what you're doing here?"

"You already know that answer to that," David's visitor told him. "What I want to know is what you're doing at Cupids Bow Ranch?"

"I'm helping out an old friend and maybe investing in a very lucrative horse breeding program," David explained.

"Sure, you are." David's visitor's eyes narrowed suspiciously. "Do you want to explain this then?" The person leaned over to the table, picked up a thick brown envelope, opened it and dumped the contents on David's bed in front of him.

David's heart froze in his chest for a second when he saw the familiar documents.

"This is not what it looks like, and you don't understand what's going on." David picked up some of the documents.

"There's also this." David's visitor pulled out some more information from the envelope. "I thought you agreed to not pursue this?"

"Like I said, it's not what it looks like." David sighed, throwing the papers on top of each other.

"I think it is very much what it looks like," David's visitor's cool eyes bore into David. "You were warned to leave this alone."

"You don't understand," David said again. "That's one of the problems with you. You're so quick to judge before you've even listened to reason."

"I judge because I've already done my homework." David's visitor leaned back in the chair. "If you think I don't understand then make me understand and prove to me I have this all wrong. Please tell me you aren't mixed up with those cousins of yours?"

"Good grief, no!" David said in disgust. "I would never. Besides, I took care of them."

"I heard," his visitor said.

"Cat!" David said as more images of the day flashed through his mind. "How is she?"

"I believe she's fine and, on her way back to Big Valley Ranch," David was assured. "The horses, including Pegasus, are back where they belong, none of them hurt. The shooter is in custody. So is his partner."

"Great," David said and rested back against the hard pillows. "What are these pillows made out of? Cement?" He tried to wiggle them soft with his head.

"If you don't stop hedging and tell me what I want to know I'm going to fill them with cement," his visitor warned him. "If you don't start talking now, David, I swear I'm going straight to Cat Sparrow with everything I have on you."

"Fine!" David lifted his hands as best he could in exasperation. "If I do tell you, will you walk away and let me finish what I've started?"

"Not, likely," his visitor said. "But you're going to tell me anyway for a chance to change my mind."

"You always were such a bully," David told him.

"I'm waiting!" his visitor said with narrowed eyes watching David.

David sighed once again, leaned back, and pinched the bridge of his nose before he started to explain.

"Are you feeling better?" Maria walked into Cat's room at Big Valley Ranch. "You look all cozy after your shower.

"Sorry, I was cold, so I put my pajamas on and hopped into bed," Cat told Maria.

"We could always do this tomorrow?" Maria put a cup of steaming cocoa on Cat's nightstand.

"No, I'm ready to hear what you have to tell me," Cat said, patting the bed next to her for Maria to sit down. "I'm tired of getting the runaround and want to know why everyone is giving it to me. I also own this land, you know?"

"I know." Maria looked down at her hands that were holding her mug of cocoa. "Indy asked me not to tell you about the inn."

"But he would've been very young when Zac was starting the inn," Cat said.

"He overheard an argument between Chelsea and Zac," Maria explained.

"Chelsea again!" Cat threw up her hand. "Why does everything that's going wrong always come back to her?" She looked at Maria.

"Maybe because it's time you forgave her?" Maria said softly.

"Have you had a chance to find those original documents you want to look for?"

"No, not yet," Cat told Maria. "I asked Janine about what happened to all the stuff in the attic of what was once my home and is now an *inn*." She emphasized the word inn.

"And was she able to tell you where they've been put?" Maria asked her.

"No, she said that only Zac would know the answer to that." Cat thoughtfully bit her lip. "I also asked Indy, Jamie, and Hayden. None of them know."

"Why haven't you asked Zac yet?" Maria pointed out the obvious. "He's the one that moved them."

"If I ask him, he's going to start asking questions that I don't want to answer," Cat said. "I'd rather avoid asking him until he is my only option."

"Which means you think you still have something up your sleeve for tracking the items down." Maria took a sip of her cocoa.

"I do." Cat nodded with a grin lighting up her face. "I have a feeling that Zac has moved the items to one of the houses he built at the back of the inn."

"That would make sense." Maria nodded. "Or he could have put them in a lock and go storage container."

"True," Cat agreed. "Zac may act like a big macho cowboy but he's very sentimental. So, he wouldn't have moved the items very far from where he was able to have access to them."

"There are some storage units close by," Maria pointed out.

"Will you stop it with the storage units?" Cat shook her head at Maria. "Trust me on this, Zac wouldn't use one of those. He'd sooner build a barn ..." She frowned as something dawned on her.

"What is it?" Maria gave Cat a knowing sideways look.

"What if Zac wasn't the one to move the stuff from the attic?" Cat looked at Maria.

"Who else would've done that?" Maria frowned. "Chelsea or Bessie?"

"No." Cat shook her head as a memory came back to her.

"Who then?" Maria asked impatiently.

"My father." Cat looked at Maria.

"Your father?" Maria looked confused. "You remember that your father is no longer with us, right?"

"Of course." Cat tutted and shook her head at Maria.

"Oh, you think he moved some of the items, like the trunks with the information you need before he left us?" Maria caught on to Cat's train of thought.

"Exactly." Cat nodded. "Two nights before my eighteenth birthday I heard a noise in the attic. Back then, I was terrified of the attic."

"I told you, you watch far too many thrillers and horror movies," Maria admonished her. "You really need to try a comedy or romance once in a while."

"I'm being serious," Cat told Maria. "When my father and I went for our traditional father-daughter birthday lunch, he gave me this."

Cat pulled her necklace with the ruby pendant from beneath her pajama top.

"Yes, you told me he'd given you that necklace," Maria reminded her.

"Yes, but what I didn't tell you is what he told me what the necklace actually was," Cat explained.

"It's not just a necklace?" Maria frowned. She leaned forward and picked up the necklace to look at it. "It is beautiful. And you're right about the weird pattern it's shaped in."

"Yes, I've often wondered about the pattern," Cat said. "But we're veering off the topic at hand."

"You always do that," Maria pointed out.

"And you were counting on it to steer the conversation away from the subject at hand," Cat told her. "So, Indy told you not to tell me about the inn when he was, what? Fifteen?"

"Something like that," Maria said. "I brought him here that one summer when Zac was waiting for you to sign off on the idea."

"Which I didn't do." Cat looked at Maria.

"Chelsea was furious when she heard that you'd once again vetoed the idea," Maria explained. "She and Zac had a huge argument. That's when Zac decided rather than lose Cupids Bow Ranch, he was going to start running the place as a bed and breakfast."

"That snake." Cat frowned.

"Cat, you don't understand how difficult things had gotten," Maria told her. "Zac didn't tell you a quarter of the problems."

"Are you sure my brother didn't create the problems?" Cat suggested. "When he was young, he had a dream of one day turning our home into a dude ranch."

"I doubt he'd sabotage his own livelihood to do something like that." Maria took another sip of her cocoa. "Like most of the ranches surrounding Cupid's Bow, Zac had to take out a mortgage on Cupids Bow just to keep up with the running costs."

"He what?" Cat's eyebrows rose as she looked at Maria in astonishment.

"Oh ..." Maria looked sheepish. "You didn't know about that either?"

"No." Cat shook her head. "But you did, and never mentioned it."

"Cat, I thought you knew." Maria frowned. "How on earth would he have gotten a mortgage without your approval?"

"That's a fine question to ask about twenty years later!" Cat said sarcastically. "I'm not sure about that, but I'm making a mental note to find out."

"You don't think he'd forge your credentials, do you?" Maria looked questioningly at Cat.

"Right now, I'd believe anything," Cat told her. "But, no, I don't think he would."

"Mm, maybe ask Ashley to look into that for you," Maria suggested.

"Ashly is annoyed with me." Cat sighed. "Like you, she suggested it was time Chelsea and I buried the hatchet."

"Does Ashley know the truth?" Maria asked her.

"No." Cat shook her head. "Only you, I, Chelsea, and the conman know about that."

"We should stop calling him the conman," Maria laughed. "One day, if I ever meet this guy, I'm probably going to blurt it out."

"Well, he is a conman. What else would you call someone who wheedles their way into a person's life for their own game?" Cat took a sip of her cocoa.

"Chelsea never told Zac either?" Maria looked surprised. "We both know what secrets like that can do to a marriage."

"Yes, I know," Cat agreed. "I think that's one of the main reasons Zac and Chelsea's marriage fell apart. Firstly, they were way too young to get married, and secondly, they were both keeping secrets from each other."

"I think Chelsea did you a favor by stealing the conman away from you," Maria said.

"Yes, I often thought that too." Cat laughed. "But before you say anything, no matter how you look at it, she betrayed me and my brother. Once again, she kept it all to herself. Chelsea wouldn't have said a word had I not stumbled across the truth."

"I'm not defending her," Maria assured Cat. "All I'm saying is that maybe, like you, she was coerced into cooperating with him."

"I don't care." Cat's eyes dulled. "I know everyone thinks that my father slipped off his saddle while trying to rehang the banner in the arena. But I know he didn't."

"After you told me your suspicions the first time, I have to agree with you," Maria backed Cat up. "I also knew that your father was a heck of a rider. Not even a ferocious bull could dismount him. There's no way he was going to slip out of a saddle."

"Also, where did he get the gash on his head that was the ultimate cause of his death?" Cat's voice got more desperate. "Judging by the way he was lying, there was nothing he could've hit his head on."

"You said he was lying half on the floor," Maria noted. "He could've hit his head then."

"No." Cat shook her head. "The gash would've been on his forehead then, because he was lying with his forehead on the floor. I could never understand why the police would rule it an accident."

"Pity we couldn't take a look at the police file," Maria said.

"I've asked Wallace to look into it," Cat told her. "He's also looking into the trouble on the ranches, as well as David."

"I don't understand why you're so suspicious of him." Maria shook her head. "He just saved your life."

"It could've all been some deliberate plan," Cat pointed out. "If he saved me then I would start to trust him. He could then manipulate me and use me to get to whatever his end game is."

"I think you're reading way too much into him looking at the pamphlet that Sally gave you." Maria put her mug down on the nightstand next to her. "Maybe he was genuinely just leafing through it. Wondering what needed to be adjusted or updated."

"Yeah," Cat nodded. "Then why did he look so guilty and try to hide the fact he'd been reading it?"

"What would you do if someone walked in and startled you?" Maria asked her. "I think what we need to do first and foremost is figure out who's leaking information about you," she said. "Today you got lucky. Tomorrow whoever wants to do you harm won't be as sloppy with their next attempt."

"What worries me the most about that is having someone I love and care about getting in the crosshairs," Cat admitted to Maria. "That's why I need to find the trunks that were in the attic of Cupids Bow house. I have this feeling that there's more to all the trouble on the ranches than we all know."

"Cat, I worry about snooping around into the past like I know you're going to do," Maria turned the conversation in another direction. "There must be another way to help Cupids Bow and save your career."

"There isn't." Cat patted Maria's hand in a reassuring manner.

"Some things just don't add up and whoever is terrorizing the five ranches seems to have been playing a long game."

"All the trouble started a little while after your father passed away," Maria pinpointed. "It was almost like once Callum was gone there was nothing or no one to keep the trouble makers at bay."

"That was the year that the cattle poaching started," Cat remembered. "It's why Zac came back to help out on his summer vacation from university."

"Yes, Brett had to come home too," Maria told her. "Losing all that cattle was the start of the decline for all five ranches. How we've all hung on to our land these past thirty-two years is a mystery."

"I knew about the poaching because I was still living at home then," Cat told her. "But I thought it had been resolved when there were no more instances that year."

"It went quiet for a year or two," Maria explained. "According to my brother, Brett, the trouble started again two years later."

"That would be right after another calving season." Cat's eyes narrowed. "They were waiting for the exact moment to strike, knowing that the ranches would only just be recovering."

"From the last loss, yes." Maria nodded in agreement. "Only Ryan Becketts older brother, Todd, managed to thwart the poachers."

"Were they caught?" Cat asked her.

"A few of them were; the main ring leaders all escaped," Maria recounted what her brother had told her. "Of course, the men the police did manage to catch weren't talking."

"Honor among thieves." Cat shook her head. "The way the ranches keep getting hit points to someone trying to cripple the ranches. A classic land grab maneuver so when the banks foreclose, the land gets auctioned off at a very low price."

"Yes, but they weren't expecting you and Aunt Simone to be able to inject cash into helping the ranches out instead of them having to take out second mortgages." Maria pulled her legs up.

"Wait a minute." Cat held up her hand. "You don't think that maybe Marshall has a hand in all this, do you?"

"No, I think that may be a bit of a stretch." Maria frowned. "But then again, didn't you say he signed the divorce without hesitation or contesting the fact he got nothing from you?"

"Yes, that made me a little suspicious because I found out he was flat broke and up to his eyeballs in gambling debts," Cat told Maria. "At first I thought maybe he was leaching off his new girlfriend, that up-and-coming new pop singing sensation."

"But now you're thinking he may have deliberately been steered in your direction?" Maria's frown deepened.

"I know it sounds far-fetched or something out of a telenovela." Cat gave a small laugh. She knew just how ludicrous someone besides Maria would think she sounded. "I've asked Wallace to look into any development projects that may be earmarked for this land."

"Development projects?" Maria's eyes widened. "You mean malls or resorts?"

"Yes." Cat nodded. "It could be for the natural forests that surround the lands. But what would they get from the trees? It's not like it's the Amazon jungle. There's not even much hunting in it. Besides, it's a reserve, so it can't really be touched."

"What about the freshwater from the river?" Maria suggested. "Water is fast becoming a big commodity."

"Again, there are other ways to get the water," Cat pointed out. "It has to be land development."

"If it is land development, whoever is behind this has really been playing a very long game," Maria said. "Surely, they would've found other places they could get a lot quicker?"

"Some development companies play it that way," Cat explained. "For instance, prime real estate that unethical developers want and don't want to pay the going price. They pay unsavory sources to start moving in around the neighborhood."

"Oh, right." Maria realized where Cat was going with this. "Families of that caliber will quickly sell up if the neighborhood is going into decline."

"Exactly, and because it's in decline, property prices drop," Cat told her. "No one wants to be living in an expensive house paying off a mortgage that's way over the value price."

"That's so wrong." Maria's eyes sparked with anger. "But if I think about it, everything that's been happening to the five ranches does seem like someone's trying to force us to sell."

"If we get too desperate, they can make any offer they like to get the land." Cat felt sick at the thought of ever having to let Cupids Bow Ranch go. "Making sure I've been discredited and then getting rid of me ensures there are no other big cash injections."

"Especially when a murder would mean no inheritances would be paid out until the investigation was over," Maria followed.

"Right," Cat confirmed. "All my assets and money would be frozen."

"Do you think that it could be possible that old man Donaldson could've been responsible for the poaching back then?" Maria put the idea out there. "You did tell me in the car that he owned a development company."

"I've been wondering that myself," Cat admitted. "Then when he passes, his nephew Ron Hicks picks up where he left off." She looked at Maria. "Do you know if any of the five ranches have been approached to sell?"

"Actually, I did ask Brett about that earlier," Maria told her. "He said that my father was approached just before my parents' airplane crash that took their lives."

Cat's eyes narrowed as a thought struck her. "Wasn't that around the same year that the Andersons lost both their parents?"

"I think you're right," Maria said. "It was also close to the time you lost your father."

"They were weakening the herd," Cat said. "I want to think that whatever is going on has to do with wanting our land, but I've got a feeling there is a lot more to it than that." She looked at Maria. "I need to find the answers if we're going to put an end to this, whatever it is, because the more I think about it the more I'm convinced my declining career was all part of some elaborate plan."

"I just wish all the answers you needed weren't in the past." Maria shuddered. "You know how I feel about dredging what has gone by. I can also remember the last time you tried to start digging into your father's death."

"I know." Cat gave her a smile. "But sometimes you have to go back to move forward."

"Yes, Cat, but the last time you started to go backward, Indy and Liam were nearly kidnapped." Maria shuddered. "Thank goodness you had a protection detail on them."

"Maria, when did all the problems on the ranches begin again?" Cat asked her.

"I'm not sure, but I'll ask Brett," Maria promised. "I'll also find out more about it."

"Thank you." Cat gave Maria's hand a squeeze. "In the meantime, I'll ask Wallace to look into Marshall's finances. Maybe something in there can give us a start."

"Although I'm thinking that's not legal, I also know right now we need all the help we can get." Maria's voice dropped. "I didn't want to worry you, but Brett can't take another loss of cattle or horses as he did last year. All the money I'm getting from my share of Simone's estate I'm putting right back into the ranch."

"I believe Chelsea is hanging onto Mountain Rise by a thread," Cat said.

"Yes," Maria confirmed. "Her mother is ill, and Chelsea has been working around the clock looking after her mother and running the ranch. She's also taken a part-time nursing job at the Lewistown clinic."

"Oh!" Cat felt a twinge of guilt at her bad thoughts about Chelsea. "I'm sorry to hear that."

"You know, Cat, while you're delving into the past, maybe it's time to let some of it go," Maria advised her.

"Maria, you know what she did." Cat's eyes flashed with a

spark of anger and her voice was laced with bitterness. "I don't know if I can ever forget that."

"Maybe start by forgiving her and listening to her side of the story," Maria said softly.

"Have you been speaking to Chelsea?" Cat's brown furrowed.

"No." Maria shook her head. "I don't know her that well only from passing and school." She looked at Cat. "I do know her mother. But only because she took over her husband's practice when he passed away and became the town doctor."

"That's right." Cat nodded. "I forgot Chelsea's parents were doctors."

"You were talking about your father moving the items from the attic," Maria went back to an earlier conversation. "Do you think you know where he moved them to?"

"I have a hunch," Cat told Maria.

But that was all Cat would say about it. She didn't know why, but for the first time since she and Maria had become friends, she found herself reluctant to share the information. Cat gave herself a mental shake. She really had become distrustful and suspicious of everyone. Maria had been nothing but a kind, caring, and loyal friend. But here Cat was suddenly suspicious of her motives for steering the conversation back to her family's secrets.

"And you're not going to tell me," Maria guessed. "That's okay. If you really think there's information in there that has all the answers to the mystery of the Sparrow family, it's best I don't know in case I'm captured and tortured."

"That's no joke, Maria," Cat said. "Look at what nearly happened to me today. Whatever is going on here, these people are no longer playing around. If the shooter is not one of Marshall's crazed fans, then he's working with whoever is behind the ranch troubles. It probably means they've reached the end of their long game."

"We'll hear from the police department tomorrow," Maria told her.

"I'm now kind of hoping that the shooter was a crazy fan,"

Cat said. "Because if he wasn't, then I'm not the only target they'll go for."

Maria gave a shudder as her wide shocked eyes met Cat's. Either way, Cat had to get whatever was going on with the ranches sorted out while getting her life back on track. Deep down, her gut was screaming at her that David was somehow in the middle of everything. This time, Cat was going to act on her intuition. The last two times she'd ignored it, she'd gotten a divorce from her first husband and her name muddied by her second divorce. There was too much at stake.

Chapter Eleven

CAT'S HOUSE ON THE RANCH

Cat hated that every sound she heard or thought she heard, was making her jump. Poor Magenta was feeling Cat's nerves, and it was getting to the horse, making her as skittish as Cat was. Wallace had warned her that it was too soon for her to go riding and that she should wait to hear back from the police about the shooter. But Cat had been determined not to become a victim. She loved riding and being out on the open plains with the wind in her hair as she and Magenta flew over the land. Sadly, Cat couldn't relax on her ride to Cupids Bow Ranch to go sit with Zac. She had a shadow following her that wasn't letting her out of his sight.

Cat was so annoyed with Maria's brother Brett for saddling Wallace up with one of his fastest horses, knowing just how speedy and agile Magenta was. Cat had told Brett to give Wallace Barney to ride, but Brett had ignored her. Barney was a lovely gelding who could be fast when he wanted to but generally, he was happy to plod along. Now instead of being able to leave Wallace in her dust, he was right behind her. Cat had wanted to take this time on her ride over to Cupids Bow to clear her mind. Something she was finding that impossible because every shadow had her heart racing. Although she'd never admit it to Wallace, he may just have been right about it being too soon for her to be out riding.

But it was too late now that they were nearly at Cupids Bow.

"Cat," Wallace called to her, "can you please slow down a bit? I need to talk to you."

Cat reigned Magenta in and turned her around to face Wallace. She was secretly glad he'd asked her to slow down and that he was with her. Cat would've probably melted into a puddle of nerves by now if she was on her own out there.

"How do you like Rover?" Cat asked Wallace as he walked the horse over to her.

"He's wonderful," Wallace said. "I do think, however, that he and Magenta are both picking up on your nervousness."

"I'm not nervous," Cat lied.

"Come on, Cat." Wallace's eyes narrowed as he stared intently at her. "You think I can't see you stiffen up every time a bird calls, or the wind blows a little gustier?"

"Fine," Cat hissed. "But can you blame me? I was shot yesterday."

"That's why I told you to let me drive you to Cupid's Bow," Wallace told her. "I wasn't trying to suffocate you as you accused me of before we left Big Valley Ranch."

"I know," Cat apologized. "There's just so much going on right now. I wanted to come home and let the freedom of the open countryside heal my wounded soul. Instead, I find my family home unrecognizable. The ranches are all hanging on by a thread, and someone wants me dead."

"I know it's a lot to process," Wallace said patiently. "I'm not trying to push you around or run your life, Cat. I'm trying to do my job as your bodyguard and I hope, your friend. That's to help you and protect you."

"I'm so glad you're here, Wallace," Cat told him honestly. "Here in Montana and on this ride with me. It's nice to have at least two people around me that I can rely on and trust."

"Cat..." Wallace looked at her. "There's something I need to tell you and I should've done as soon as I got to Montana."

"Okay..." Cat frowned, wondering what he wanted to tell her. Although she'd often spoken to him, Wallace had told her very little about his family or life.

"Before I came to Montana, I ran a full background check on everyone working at all five of the ranches that you would visit or be near," Wallace began telling her.

"Uh-oh," Cat said, not liking the look on his face. "Is this where you tell me I have to pack up and go within the hour?" She tried to lighten the mood that had suddenly become intense.

"No." Wallace shook his head and gave a soft laugh. "Or at least not yet."

"Good," Cat breathed. "Because there's still a lot of unsolved business for us to do here."

"About that," Wallace started to tell her what he wanted to do once again, but they were interrupted by the sound of a horse approaching.

Cat instantly stiffened and turned Magenta so suddenly she nearly made her rear.

"Whoa," Wallace grabbed the side of Magenta's reins when she started to object to Cat's abrupt command. "Steady, girl."

Wallace gently stroked Magenta's cheek to calm her.

"Sorry," Cat said, her heart pounding in her ears as they watched the rider approach. "Is that David?" She stared in amazement as David rode Clive towards them.

"Hi," David waved.

"What on earth are you doing out of the hospital?" Cat asked him, eyeing out his arm that was in a sling. "How can you even ride with cracked and bruised ribs?"

"I'm tough, I can take it." David grinned and tipped his hat at Wallace in a greeting. "Zac told me you were riding out to Cupids Bow this morning. I wanted to come and make sure you were okay."

"As you can see," Wallace's voice was cool and controlled, "Cat is fine and perfectly safe."

"Is she?" David held his ground with Wallace. "Where were you yesterday when she was being shot at?"

"Investigating certain unscrupulous people that may be trying to ruin Cat and her family's reputation as well as steal their land." Wallace looked pointedly at David.

What was going on here? Cat wondered. Her instincts started to send little warning signals to her as the undertones of Wallace and David's conversation didn't go amiss by her. Cat watched the interactions between the two men closely and she wondered if they somehow knew each other. Maybe that's what Wallace was trying to tell her when David interrupted Wallace's conversation.

"Thank you, David, for caring, but you shouldn't be out riding or even out of the hospital," Cat told him. "But I'm perfectly safe with Wallace. I trust him with my life."

"That's good to know." David gave Wallace a tight smile. "Now that I'm here, I'll ride along."

"Great," Wallace said through clenched teeth.

The three of them took off towards Cupid's Bow Ranch.

An hour after David's visitor at the hospital had left the previous day, the doctor had come to see him. David had insisted that he be released, and the doctor had reluctantly signed him out. He knew it was probably a bad move, but he'd been shot before when he was in the military and a couple of hours later, he was back out on patrol. The doctor had pointed out that David had been a lot younger back then, but he'd been determined to go. David had a suspicion that his last hospital visitor was about to blow his world up around him, and he had to try to stop it.

David knew that Cat was scheduled to spend the morning at Zac's house. He'd called Big Valley Ranch, and Maria told him that Cat was riding to Cupids Bow Ranch. David had a hunch that she wouldn't be riding alone after the previous day. It turned out his hunch was correct. While David, Cat, and her bodyguard rode towards Cupid's Bow Ranch, he wondered just how much the man knew about everyone within a hundred-mile radius of

Cat. What David wondered about the most was how much of what the man knew he had already told Cat. This was going to cause a problem for him.

As Clive galloped alongside Cat and her bodyguard, David's ribs ached with every one of the horse's movements. His arm, where he'd had a bullet removed, was on fire, and his head was starting to pound. But David ignored the nausea rising up from his stomach and all the pain, determined not to let Cat's bodyguard see any weakness in him. He'd never been as happy to see Cupids Bow Ranch appear as he was then. When they reached the ranch David had really wanted to stick around to try to find out how much Cat knew, but he was feeling really bad. His ribs, head, and both places he'd had bullets removed were killing him.

"David, you're bleeding!" Cat pulled Magenta up next to him when they stopped by the Cupids Bow stables.

"I'm sure it's nothing." David smiled, hoping that it didn't look forced.

"I'm calling Liam." Cat pulled out her phone and dialed.

"I'm sure it's nothing, please don't worry him. I know he's just come off a full day shift at the hospital," David told her.

But it was too late. Cat was already talking to Liam and, by the sound of the conversation, Liam was already on his way to them. This was all he needed. An 'I told you so' from Liam and a 'what were you thinking' from Cat's smug bodyguard.

"You shouldn't be riding," Wallace said to David, sliding off his horse and handing the reins to the stable hand. "Thank you," he told the young man who nodded and walked Rover off. "Can I give you a hand?" He looked up at David.

Two other stable hands came to tend to Clive and Magenta.

"No, I'm good," David lied.

He watched Cat slide easily off her horse before he gathered all the energy he could muster and dismounted. When his feet hit the ground, pain ricocheted through his body making him see spots in front of his eyes. David drew in deep breaths, trying to push away the swirling gray mists that made him feel cold from his feet up to his brain.

"Whoa, buddy," David heard Wallace say before he felt a hand on the forearm that wasn't in the sling.

"I'm good," David lied again, holding up his hand and swallowing down the pain. "But I think I will lie down for a while. If you'll excuse me."

"Yeah, you're coming with me," Liam appeared in front of David. "I told you this was going to happen."

"Don't be smug," David told Liam. "I was worried about Cat."

"Sure, you were," Wallace said softly to him, making David glare at him as best he could with a pounding headache. "I'll help you get him to your house," he said to Liam.

"I can walk there on my own," David said, feeling like an idiot in front of Cat.

"Why don't you two back off?" Cat looked from Liam to Wallace. "I'll help David to Liam's house if that's where we're going. It's my fault. David was only looking out for me."

"It's not your fault, Cat." David gave her the biggest smile he could muster at the moment. "There's a lot that's been going on here and I think we may all just be targets." He couldn't believe he'd just said that.

"I was thinking the same thing," Cat told him, stepping up beside him and putting his good arm around her. "Here, lean on me."

David's heart skidded and then skipped a few beats like a stone skipping over smooth, glassy water. Except, instead of sinking, his heart felt like it was going to float out of his chest when her small arm wrapped around his waist and her warm body supported him.

"I might crush you," David worried.

"Nah," Cat gave a soft laugh. "I'm a lot stronger than I look," she assured him as they started to make their way to the house with Liam and Wallace following close behind them.

"What were you saying before about thinking we were all targets?" David asked her.

He was trying his best not to wince with every step they took and he was careful not to put too much weight on her.

"Last night, Maria was telling me everything she knew about what was going on with all the trouble the five ranches in this area have been having," Cat explained. "Yesterday, I thought that the shooter might be a crazed fan of my ex-husband who's causing trouble for me." She steered him around some uneven ground. "But then, when I thought a little more about it, I realized that it could be some sort of land-grab type ploy."

"What made you draw that conclusion?" David asked her curiously, feeling a little alarmed at just how shrewd Cat was.

"It's just something my daddy told me a few days before he died," was all Cat told him, and he wasn't going to raise her suspicions by pushing her.

But David was now really curious to find out just how much Callum Sparrow had known about what was going on around him. Guilt surged through David as he glanced down at Cat. She was beautiful, talented, and very smart. She'd also haunted his dreams since the day he'd followed her into the stables at her father's funeral. David knew the moment he'd laid eyes on her that she was the girl of his dreams. But fate truly was a cruel master. Because he knew she'd never be his and when he'd finally found what he was looking for she'd probably hate him. David was going to lose both his best friend and the woman who'd stolen his heart when she was eighteen. David's heart went from flying high at being so close to Cat to falling to his ankles, deflated.

"Are you okay?" Cat's voice pulled him from his musings.

"Yes." David gave her a weak smile. "I'm trying hard not to give in to the pain or admit to just how much of it I'm in right now."

Cat gave a small laugh and shook her head at him, "You're only human, David, and even big strong men are allowed to ask for help when they need it. It's not a weakness, it's a strength knowing when to reach out."

"You're just full of wisdom today, aren't you?" David teased her. "I was really worried about you," he told her honestly.

"I have Wallace," Cat pointed out.

"Where was he yesterday when you needed him the most, though?" David asked her. "He should've been with you, Cat."

"You can't blame Wallace," Cat told him. "I had asked him to do something important for me."

"Couldn't he have done what you asked him to do when he knew you weren't vulnerable?" David knew it wasn't his place, but he couldn't help feeling overly protective of her.

"Who would've suspected that I'd be in danger on my own property?" Cat looked up at him. "Besides, you were with me."

"A lot of good that did us," David laughed.

"You saved my life, David." Cat looked up at him with admiration shining in her eyes, making the guilt claw through his gut.

"Actually, I think it was Pegasus that saved all three of our lives," David pointed out.

"I know. What an amazing horse he is!" Cat breathed.

"They used to use them as war horses when battles were still fought with swords, arrows, and other weapons besides guns." David sighed.

"You sound like you're a fan of ancient-type battles?" Cat looked up at him again.

"While I was in the army, I went to an old war museum with some of my team," David told her. "They had an entire history of the weapons used in war through the ages."

"My brother didn't happen to be one of those team members, did he?" Cat asked him. "Because Zac has always been enthralled with historical wars."

"Actually, he was with me," David confirmed. "Come to think of it, it was his idea to go to the museum. We had a day pass while we were crossing Europe and stopped off in London."

"I didn't know Zac has been to London." Cat's brows furrowed.

"You know I can't talk about why we were in Europe. I can only talk about our day pass," David told her.

"Fair enough." Cat stopped when they got to Liam's house. "I'm afraid you're going to have to let those two help you up the stairs."

"It's okay." David smiled. "I think I can make it on my own."

"I don't think so," Liam said, stepping up next to David. "Come on, old-timer." He grinned cheekily at David's glare. "Let's get you to the spare room."

"I'm only accepting your help because I know you're going to force it on me anyway." David put his arm around Liam's shoulders for support. "And I'm in no condition to fight you off."

"Let's go with that." Liam nodded and helped David up the stairs. "I'll let you know how he is once I've watched him up and got him lying down," he called over his shoulder, leading David to the front door.

"Sedate him if you have to," David heard Wallace advise Liam, and it made him instantly angry.

"I'll check in on you later, David," Cat called after them.

David turned his head and smiled at Cat. He also saw the narrowed-eyed stare Wallace was giving him but chose to ignore the man and let Liam lead him inside.

"That was so sweet of David," Cat said to Wallace as they watched Liam lead David into the house.

"Just how much do you know about David Miller?" Wallace asked her.

"I know that my brother trusts him and has been friends with him for many years," Cat told Wallace. "I also know that he came to help my brother out of a tight spot when the previous Cupids Bow Ranch foreman was arrested."

"We need to talk," Wallace told her. "I would suggest a ride, but after yesterday I think it's best we stick closer to the ranch."

"I've been wanting to look in my new house." Cat pointed to the house opposite Zac's. "Let me get the keys and make sure Zac's okay, then we can go talk in there."

"Great," Wallace said, following Cat to Zac's front door. "While you're sorting out Zac, I want to go and check on the horses. I also want to do some quick digging into who knew you and David were going to the south fields yesterday."

"You think someone here is leaking information?" Cat's eyes widened.

"It was no coincidence that the shooter was waiting for you and David near those fields," Wallace pointed out. "The fence had also been strategically cut knowing that David would stop around that exact area to inspect it."

"Great." Cat threw up her hands. "Now I feel even less secure on my own land."

"Sorry, Cat. That wasn't my intention," Wallace told her. "But at least now you'll be a little more vigilant. If you see anything you think is out of the ordinary, I need to know."

"Of course," Cat nodded. "I'll wait in the house until you get back."

"Good." Wallace gave her a nod. "I would also feel a lot happier if I came in and did a quick sweep of the house."

"I think I would feel better if you did as well," Cat agreed and let herself into Zac's house. "Zac, I'm here," she called.

"Hi, Cat," Zac shouted from his room. "I'm so glad you're here. I've dropped the remote control and I want to watch the news."

"On my way." Cat shook her head. "I'll leave you to look around."

Wallace gave her another nod and quietly went about checking the house while Cat went through to Zac's room.

"Do you need anything else before I go and look around my new house?" Cat said enthusiastically.

She didn't want Zac to think she had an ulterior motive for wanting to look around the house.

"No, I should be fine, and I have my phone if I need

anything." Zac picked up his phone to show her. "Besides, I want to watch the news, and you know I love watching it uninterrupted."

"I do." Cat nodded. "Oh, Zac, what happened to all the stuff that was in the attic up at the ranch house?"

"I'm not sure," Zac frowned. "I remember there were a lot of old trunks and books. But when I went to get it moved to the storehouse those were all gone. There were only bits of furniture, and clothes, along with some of mom and dad's personal stuff."

"That's strange," Cat said. "Do you think that dad might have had the stuff moved?"

"I don't know." Zac shook his head. "I've been looking for them. I thought that maybe there'd be a copy of the land deed for the ranch in one of the trunks. But they all seemed to have just vanished."

"You've kept the old storeroom?" Cat asked him.

"Yes." Zac nodded. "I've even left dad's office above it intact." He smiled. "I never had the heart to touch it. I have it cleaned once a week and I've made it my secret retreat."

"Do you mind if I go look around there?" Cat looked at Zac.

"Cat, this is your home too," Zac pointed out. "You can go wherever you please." He smiled. "I keep the keys locked away though."

"Oh," Cat said. "Is that in the same place where you've locked my keys?"

"Yes," Zac confirmed. "There are just a few places on the farm that I don't want people to go nosing about."

"Good thinking," Cat told him. "I promise to not let anyone else get the keys," she teased him.

"There are some memories that are worth preserving and sometimes you have to lock them away to make sure they are safe," Zac told her. "Everything that I've physically locked away is protecting our family's history and memory. I feel that it's important for our kids and the future generations of Sparrows to know their history."

"You and your history." Cat laughed. "I'll be back to check up on you. Call me if you need anything; I'll be nosing around the ranch."

"Nose away, little sister." Zac grinned before turning on the television, which Cat took as a sign that it was time for her to leave the room.

"Simple but elegant," Cat said, looking around the house Zac had built for her.

"I think it's beautiful." Wallace gave a low whistle. "It looks similar to Zac's house from the outside, but the inside it's completely different."

"It's the house I designed for myself when my father told Zac and me what he wanted to do for us one day." Cat smiled. "My daddy told us to design our perfect house. I drew this one."

Cat and Wallace took a tour of the ground floor, the first floor, and the second floor, and then Cat braved the attic with Wallace. But the attic was completely empty. It was also light and airy, which Cat assumed was due to Zac knowing how much Cat hated dark attics.

"You could do a lot with this space," Wallace said, looking around the room. "I like how Zac has made it so bright."

"Yes, he knows I can't stand dark rooms, especially attics," Cat told Wallace.

"Being around you and your family has made me miss my father," Wallace told her.

"You should go and visit him," Cat told him. "Where does he live?"

"Before we get to chatting about me," Wallace politely changed the subject, Cat noted, "we need to talk about a few people."

"Okay." Cat led them out of the attic. "Why don't we go sit in the living room?"

Wallace followed Cat down the stairs and into the living

room. Cat took a seat in one of the stylish armchairs while Wallace sat on a sofa.

"What have you found out?" Cat asked him.

"You're not going to like it," Wallace warned her. "Especially the parts about your new best friend, David Miller."

"He's not my best friend." Cat's brow creased. "But I do owe him for saving my life."

David reached into his jacket pocket and pulled out a fat A5 envelope, which he handed to Cat. "This will explain everything you need to know about the Cupids Bow Ranch foreman."

Cat's frown deepened, and her heart raced looking down at the envelope in her hand. Part of her wanted to burn the information in the envelope so she never saw what it was. Cat knew her fascination with David had been restarted the moment she'd seen him at the Billings airport when she'd arrived back in Montana. She hadn't been able to get him off her mind. No matter what she was doing, he always seemed to be present in her thoughts.

After yesterday, when he had saved her life, Cat was actually beginning to trust him and had wanted to call Wallace's investigation into David off. But the more rational part of her brain had stopped her. Now, here she sat holding what she could only imagine was damaging information about David in her hands.

"Can you give me a summary of what's in here?" Cat looked at Wallace.

"Okay." Wallace leaned back on the sofa and started to tell Cat what was in the envelope.

When Wallace was finished telling Cat about David, he went on to tell her that the shooter wasn't associated with Cat's ex-husband, Marshall Myers. He was an associate of Ron Hicks Junior, who was Ron Hicks senior's eldest son. Ryan's ranch hand was the husband of Stacy Hicks, Ron Hicks senior's daughter.

"Wouldn't Ryan have done a thorough background check on his staff?" Cat stopped Wallace mid-sentence.

It was bugging Cat how the ranch hand could've been working right under Ryan's nose, and he didn't know the man was married to a Hicks. It was also a way to keep her mind from snapping back to what Wallace had told her about David. Cat didn't want to think about that until she was alone and could process it. She didn't want Wallace to see the hurt, anger, and disbelief that was bubbling up inside her. So, Cat decided to steer the conversation in another direction.

"The guy is the son of one of the hands that have worked for the Becketts for many years," Wallace explained. "Ryan's ranch foreman hired him because of who the guy's father was."

"But still," Cat frowned. "I know Ryan and he would run a background check on his own family if he had to."

"I did notice how paranoid Ryan Beckett is," Wallace said. "I know that he's currently looking into his ranch foreman and everyone else who works for him after this episode."

"Ryan also hates disloyalty." Cat sighed and shook her head. "I feel sorry for anyone else he finds that's working for what he'd class as an enemy."

"I know he did quite a few tours when he was in the rangers," Wallace told her. "But he doesn't seem to show any signs of PTSD."

"No, Ryan had always just been suspicious," Cat said. "We used to tease him that he ran background checks on anyone new at school or in Lewistown." She laughed.

"How would he get his hands on information like that at such a young age?" Wallace asked, surprised.

"Ah, so you haven't done that deep a dive into the Becketts?" Cat smiled at Wallace. "The Becketts are not only ranches, but their father and grandfather before were all Lewistown's police captains."

"That's right." Wallace nodded. "Their mother was the local florist and that explained the flowers Four Lakes grows."

"Oh, yes," Cat said. "You should see Four Lakes in the springtime." She smiled. "When their mother died, Ryan's sister, Gwen, took up her mother's flower business."

Wallace looked at his watch. "Are you going to be okay for a couple of hours?" He looked at her. "Or do you want to come with me to the police station?"

"No." Cat shook her head. Without Wallace here she could go explore the storeroom, and it would give her time to think about the information she'd learned regarding David. "I'll stay with Zac, so I'll be fine, and I'll even lock the front door."

"Good," Wallace nodded, getting up.

Cat also got up and led him out of her house. She turned and locked the front door before letting Wallace walk her to Zac's house. Cat stood back and let Wallace do a quick sweep of the house before he left for the police station in Zac's car. Before he left, he'd taken Cat aside to tell her one last bit of information he thought she needed to know. What he told her had left her speechless and not quite sure of what to say. Wallace told her that she now had a decision to make and, no matter what her decision might be, he'd understand. He acknowledged that he should've told her a long time ago and not kept it a secret.

Chapter Twelve

THE DREAM

Cat made sure Zac was comfortable and didn't need anything. He was watching some Spanish telenovela that he admitted he'd got hooked on over the past few days of being in bed. So, Cat left him to it while she went to explore the storeroom. She was sure her father had hidden the chests and books somewhere in there. Cat thought that maybe there was even a secret room that they weren't aware of, where he could've put them. But her mind kept coming back to why her father would want to hide the stuff in the first place.

The back garden of Zac's house cleverly enclosed the storeroom, which ensured that only he had access to it. Other than the windows high up on the wall that faced the back of Zac's house, the only other windows in the storeroom were the ones in their father's office. Cat's heart felt sad and heavy as she stood looking up at her father's office. It had been almost thirty-two years and she still missed him terribly. Cat shook off her sadness and let herself into the building. She switched on the lights as she walked into it. Since she was still feeling uneasy after what had happened the previous day, she locked the door behind her.

While Cat looked around the storeroom, her mind ticked over the conversation she'd had with Wallace about David. Anger instantly started to warm her veins as she thought about what she now knew. Cat was beginning to think she'd misjudged David, but it turned out her instincts had been spot on. He was as big a shark as the people who were trying to drive them off their land her family had been a part of for generations. In fact, the Sparrows had been on their land before Lewistown was developed. Back when the town was still a Shawnee Native American Village called Ohesson in the mid-sixteen-hundreds.

By the time Cat had finished searching every inch of the storeroom, she had to admit defeat. There were no trap doors, and the cellar was just that, a cellar complete with ancient bottles of wine. Cat shuddered thinking of how acidic those wines must taste now. She made a mental note to talk to Zac about selling them as they were worth a pretty penny. Especially if the ranch needed cash flow. It was ridiculous what wine connoisseurs would pay for rotten ancient wine. Cat could never understand why though; it wasn't as if they were ever going to drink it.

Cat sighed and looked around the storeroom one last time. There must be something somewhere leading to a clue where her father had stashed those old trunks and books. Cat looked at the stairs that led up to the office. She had deliberately left the office for last because she knew how it was going to affect her. Cat took a deep breath and bravely walked up the stairs, reminding herself she'd survived a shooting. Well, she hadn't actually been shot, but she'd been shot at.

Cat took another deep breath, reaching for the door handle and forcing herself to open it. She stepped inside and felt tears immediately spring to her eyes. Zac hadn't been lying when he'd said he had left the office exactly as their father had left it. Although Cat figured Zac, being the obsessive neat freak he was, had cleaned the desk. Their father's desk never looked that clean. It was always cluttered with books, papers, and so on. Cat walked over to the large antique desk, running her fingers over the wood. She could remember all the times as a child sitting here while her father worked. He'd always give Cat a pencil and paper so she could pretend to be working as well.

Cat scanned the office, moved cabinets, and tried to find some hidden compartment, but there was nothing. The building was just one solid mass with no secret chambers. Cat flopped into her father's old leather office chair behind his desk and looked out the window. Her father had loved to sit here looking through the large windows because he could see the stables and paddocks. Now all you could see was the back of Zac's house. Cat felt deflated.

"Daddy, where on earth did you put all the stuff from the attic?" Cat sighed.

She pulled her pendant that was always tucked beneath her shirt out and sat looking at it. "So, necklace, how are you supposed to unlock the past to explain what the heck is going on?"

Cat leaned back in the chair, tilting her head up, and examining the pendant. She flipped it over to look at the back like she had done a million times, and that was when saw something etched on it. She frowned and pulled the piece of jewelry closer to her eyes, but she couldn't see it too well. Cat sat forward and switched on the desk lamp, but it wasn't strong enough. She looked through the desk draws for a flashlight, finding one that she knew must be Zac's because it was one of those ultramodern ones that could change to a black light. Why on earth would he need a black light?

Cat leaned back against the chair like she was when she spotted the pattern on the back of her pendant. She held the necklace up with the ruby facing the roof so she could shine the light on it and found the inscription, *buscar*!

"Buscar?" Cat scrunched up her eyes and tried to look closer. "I know the Spanish word buscar." She sat staring up at the pendant with a deep frown creasing her brow. "Look? Search?"

Her finger accidentally flipped the switch, turning the light to UV. Cat's eyes widened in amazement when she saw a drawing come alive on the office ceiling. "Look up!" She muttered, dropping the pendant. "Oh, my word."

Cat pushed herself into a standing position to run the flashlight over the ceiling. She realized the pattern drawn on it was a map of the Snowy Mountains that border the ranch. A memory of a hike she, Zac, and their father had gone on crossed her mind. They were never allowed to go into the mountains without their father. It was one of the only rules Callum Sparrow enforced on them. He'd never told them why other than that some paths were better not walked, especially if a person was not ready or equipped to walk them. Zac and Cat had never questioned their father about it. When they were growing up, they may have defied their parents on a lot of things but never the mountain.

"Why do you have a secret drawing of the mountains on your ceiling, daddy?" Cat asked softly. "Why do you have that tiny inscription on the pendant?"

Cat flopped back into the office chair, drumming her fingers on the desk as she tried to remember the one time their father had taken them into the mountains. Cat had been fourteen and Zac seventeen. It was summertime, but the mountain had still been freezing. It was one of the most memorable things about that hike for Cat. She knew they'd spend the night up there, but she couldn't remember camping.

Cat sighed, feeling frustrated. A mountain hike wouldn't lead her to the trunks anyway. But she was still curious as to why her father had a secret map of the mountains. What it did not explain to her was why Zac had a UV light flashlight in the office. Her eyes narrowed as she tapped the flashlight against her hand, thinking. Cat wasn't sure the inscription had anything to do with the drawing on the ceiling. There was no way her father would ever think she could've figured that out. No, it had been a coincidence that Cat had found the inscription while looking at the pendant.

Cat was back at square one, still none the wiser as to where the trunks were. She sat swiveling the chair from side to side, feeling frustrated. How was she supposed to unlock the past if she could freakin' find anything to unlock? Cat stifled a yawn. She had hardly slept the previous night because of her ordeal that day. She knew she wasn't going to sleep well for the next few nights. Especially now that her mind was racing with the information about David. The worst thing was that Cat couldn't even have a showdown with him right now. She had to wait until he was a little stronger at least. Then there was Wallace. What was she going to do about him? Cat wasn't even sure where to begin with that situation. Her head started to ache. Cat rubbed her temples, leaned her head back against the soft leather, and closed her eyes while she tried to massage the pain away.

THIRTY-SIX YEARS AGO

"Daddy, when are we going to stop for a rest?" fourteen-year-old Cat grumbled. "It's freezing up here."

"That's because summer is not fully here yet, Kitty Cat," Callum Sparrow told his daughter. "Do you want to climb on my back for a little while? The path is not that steep for the next couple of miles."

"Miles?" Cat looked at her father in disgust. "I thought we weren't even allowed in the mountains because they were sacred or something."

"Yes, miles." Callum laughed at the look on her face. "I told you and Zac that only when you're ready to come up here you could," he corrected her. "Mainly because the mountains can be treacherous, especially to someone who doesn't know or understand them."

"How do you understand mountains?" Cat's young brow frowned. "They're just massive rocks rising up from the land."

"Oh, Kitty Kat, they are so much more than that." Callum sighed. "So do you want me to give you a lift on my back?"

"No, dad." Zac jogged back down to them. He had hiked a little ways ahead because Cat had slowed down and started to moan. Zac had said she sounded like an annoying buzz saw with all her whining. "I'll carry her."

He walked over to his sister and handed his father his backpack. "Come on, your whiney highness."

"I'm not whining." Cat glared at Zac. "I'm just not used to the altitude."

"We're barely off the ground," Zac pointed out and turned his back towards her. "Now climb on and let's get moving. Dad wants to be on the other side of the mountain before nightfall or we have to camp on the mountain tonight."

"The other side of the mountain?" Cat gaped at her father. "No one said anything about going over the top of that mountain." She looked up. "That will take days, not a few hours!"

"Oh, Kitty Cat." Callum sighed again and shook his head. "You used to be so adventurous before you became a teenager."

"I'm still adventurous, daddy," Cat told him, hopping onto her brother's back. "Only now I'm more cautious and choosier about the adventures I embark on."

"Embark on?" Zac mocked. "You sound like a pirate about to head out onto the high seas."

"And you sound like a geek that reads too many history books," Cat slammed his sarcasm back at him. "Now giddy up, horsey, let's conquer this mountain."

Cat kicked Zac in the sides like she was spurring on her horse, Zeus.

"Do that again and I'll drop you on your butt," Zac warned her.

"Daddy, did you hear that?" Cat turned to look at their father. "Zac threatened me."

"Stop it, both of you," Callum warned them, walking ahead to lead the way. "Or I'll leave you both here to sort it out on your own."

"Great," Cat said. "I think that would fall under the category of child abuse."

"Stop antagonizing dad," Zac warned her. "Let's crack on with this hike. I'm dying to see the cabin we're staying in."

"I hope it has hot and cold running water as well as a bathroom indoors," Cat said.

"Dad's right, Kitty Cat, you really have become a teenage brat." Zac laughed when Cat swatted him on the back of the head.

They walked for another few miles along a wide ledge of the mountain until they came to an area that was blocked by a huge boulder. Cat slid off Zac's back and stood looking at the blocked path with her father and brother.

"Now what are we going to do?" Zac looked at their father questioningly.

"You see this is why only those who know the mountains can walk them," Callum told them in one of his lesson time voices. "Look closely at what you both see as a blockage."

Cat and Zac stood examining the huge boulder that was bigger than all three of them as well as taller.

"We're going to go over it?" Zac asked Callum.

"Nope!" Callum shook his head. "Come on you two, what have I taught you both your entire lives?"

"What? Do you mean other than how adults have a lot of rules they like to lay down but never follow themselves?" Cat grinned cheekily at her father. "Ooh, wait." She held up her hand. "How about 'do as I say, not as I do!'?"

"Cat!" Zac hissed at her and shook his head before turning to their father. "Nothing is ever as it seems or as bad as it first looks."

"Oh, that!" Cat made a face.

"That's right, Zac." Callum patted him on the back. "Now keep that thought in mind and look at the boulder again."

"Is it going to magically morph into a portal that will transport us to the other side of the mountain?" Cat asked her father, giving him an angelic smile when he gave her a black look.

"Cat, be serious," Callum told her. "There's a reason for everything I teach you and your brother. One day, you'll understand and be guided by it."

"Sorry, daddy," Cat said, looking contrite. "Please continue the lesson."

Callum rolled his eyes and shook his head. "Okay, smart

mouth," he said to Cat. "See if you can figure out how we're going to get around this rock." He saw Cat was about to say something and cut her off, "And, no, it doesn't change into a magical portal."

"That's boring," Cat told him. "Okay, rock, what are you hiding?"

"Can I help her, dad?" Zac asked their father.

"Of course," Callum told him. "In the meantime, I'm going to have a seat on this rock here and eat an apple. You have until I'm finished eating to figure it out."

"Oh goodie," Cat said. "Now we're being timed by an apple."

"Cat," Zac hissed. "Come on, we can figure this out."

"Sure, we can," Cat nodded. "There's a giant rock plopped in our path, and we have to figure out how to somehow get around ..." Her eyes widened. "This rock was deliberately put here."

"What are you talking about?" Zac asked her and then saw what she was seeing. "You're right. It's not like those other rocks on the mountain at all."

"Which means ..." Cat looked at Zac, excitement shining in her eyes.

"It's been put here to hide something," Zac grinned.

"Like maybe a cave?" Cat's eyes widened. "But how do we get it to move out of the way?"

"We don't," Zac told her. "What does dad always say?"

"When nothing down below makes sense, look up!" Cat jumped up and down clapping her hands. "So, if we have to look up..." She and Zac scanned the rock shelf above the boulder.

"There!" Zac pointed to the side of the mountain that ran up next to the boulder. "There is a shelf just above the boulder."

"That's why we have the climbing gear with us," Cat nodded as realization dawned on her.

"Look up there," Zac showed her. "There are carabiners, those closed hooks used to secure rope."

"Cool," Cat said. "Should I go up first?" She looked up at her brother.

"Yeah, right." Zac raised an eyebrow, looking at her. "Because you're strong enough to pull me and then dad up there."

"Oh, right!" Cat nodded. "I guess you're it then."

"I guess so," Zac said, he turned around to tell their father, but Callum was gone. "Dad?"

Cat spun around. Her excitement faded away and a gripping fear started to claw at her belly when she saw their father was no longer sitting eating his apple on the rock.

"Daddy!" Cat cupped her hands over her mouth to call out for their father. "Maybe he went to the bathroom."

"No." Zac shook his head and his eyes narrowed when they fell on their father's knife sticking in the ground pinning a note.

See you on the other side. Don't touch anything and let the lights guide your way. Remember everything I taught you about the natural beauty you find in nature.

"He wrote all that while we were figuring out the rock?" Cat looked skeptical. "Maybe he's been kidnapped and had to write it in duress." She looked around the mountain. "Or there is a magic portal to the other side of the mountain."

"Or another way!" Zac's brows furrowed. "He said that everything he's ever taught us was for a reason and one day we'll understand and be guided by it."

"I hate it when he talks in riddles," Cat said through gritted teeth. "He also took our backpacks. All he left us were some flashlights, jackets, and two apples."

"He can be such a crazy coot sometimes!" Zac said, frustratedly, he suddenly stopped talking as he looked down. "Everything he taught us was for a reason." He started to laugh.

"Are you hysterical?" Cat gave her brother a sideways glance. "Do you need me to slap you?"

"No, don't you dare," Zac warned her. "Look." He pointed to the ground. "Dad's footprints lead directly into that rock."

"Ohhhh," Cat said, following her brother's train of thought. "That rock and the hooks are a decoy."

"Exactly," Zac nodded. "The real opening is somewhere in this part of the mountain."

"Clever," Cat said and sighed. "Why can't anything ever be easy?" She looked at Zac. "I think everything should be like a computer game. When you reach something like this a little neon sign pops up saying, 'try this entrance'."

"Come on Minnie moaner," Zac said, picking up the jackets, flashlights, and fruit. "We're obviously going to need these. So put this on now." He handed her a jacket.

"Okay," you didn't have to ask her twice right now to put a warm, puffer coat on. She was freezing.

Cat slipped into the coat, "It was nice of him though to take our stuff for us. I was getting sore shoulders carrying that heavy pack. I'm not the one wanting to join the military. That would be you."

"Agh." Zac rolled his eyes again. "Can you stop moaning and help me figure out where the heck dad went?"

"Sure." Cat sighed. "But I really need that apple. I'm starved."

"You're always hungry." Zac shook his head and gave her an apple. "Now let's figure this out."

"Can I see dad's note again?" Cat asked Zac.

"Here," Zac handed Cat the note.

"Don't touch anything." Cat stared at the rock face in front of them. "Do you remember when dad took us to the ice caves?"

"Yes." Zac stood next to her and looked at what she was looking at. "What are you thinking?"

"We went with that friend of his who was one of the ice cave guides." Cat tilted her head looking at the rock.

"I do remember that." Zac looked at her. "We went to a part no one else was allowed to go to. It was really cool."

"Dad said, '*Don't touch anything and let the lights guide your way. Remember everything I taught you about the natural beauty you find in nature,'* the exact thing he wrote here." Cat pointed out.

"That's right." Zac's eyes widened. "There was a small hidden opening that a grown man the size of that extra-large guide could just squeeze through."

"We had to crawl on our hands and knees to get through the tunnel until it opened into a cavern." Cat started to feel along the rock wall. "I was scared because I don't like small dark spaces."

"I had to help you through it, but there were also tiny sparkles of light from the gemstones," Zac remembered.

They looked for any small opening but couldn't find one. Cat plopped herself on the rock their father was sitting on and rested her chin on her knees.

"That's just great we're going to be stranded on the mountain and eaten by mountain goats," Cat muttered

"This isn't Switzerland," Zac told her. "There are no mountain goats. Besides, they don't eat humans, but wolves, coyotes, and mountain lions do."

"Wonderful." Cat threw up her hands. "We're predator bait."

"Relax, little sister," Zac sat next to her and when he did, the rock wobbled.

Cat and Zac both looked wide-eyed at each other, and then down at the rock they were sitting on.

"Dad said he was going to sit on this rock right here." Cat pointed to the rock they were on.

Zac shook his head and closed his eyes for a second, "Unbelievable," he hissed. "Don't you ever just wish he could teach us a normal lesson instead of making us learn the hard way?"

"I say that all the time," Cat pointed out. "You're the suck-up who always sticks up for him." She nodded. "I love him dearly." She looked at Zac. "But when he does things like this, I want to strangle him."

"I get it," Zac nodded then blew out a breath. "So, are we going to see what's behind this rock?"

"I guess so," Cat said. "We don't know our way home, so I guess the only way really is through."

Zac nodded and stood up, pulling Cat up when she reached

out both her hands. "You're so lazy." He laughed at her. "Ready?" He crouched down ready to move the rock and Cat nodded.

Zac didn't have to push the rock very hard until it slid to the side. Behind it was a small hole on the rock's surface.

"Great, another dark hole in the mountain I have to crawl through," Cat said, shaking her head. "Well, let's get this over with."

Cat crawled into the small opening and waited for Zac. Because she was small, she could turn around to watch him crawl in. "Zac you have to pull the rock closed. Look, there's a type of handle on it."

"So, there is." Zac was bigger than Cat and couldn't turn. "You're going to have to reach over me and pull it. It's not heavy."

"That's because I don't think it's a real rock," Cat pointed out.

Cat reached over her brother and pulled the rock back into place. It made a click as it slid neatly into place.

"Do you want me to go first?" Zac asked her.

"Yes, that would be good," Cat nodded, sliding around him so he could go first. "That way you get to be eaten by the goat first."

"I told you there are no goats here and they don't eat people." Zac shook his head. "Come on, let's go find our whacky father."

"Yeah, how can he just leave us there to starve?" Cat muttered as she crawled behind her brother.

"Cat, you are right on top of me," Zac grunted when she accidentally crawled onto his feet.

"Sorry," Cat said, but didn't back away. There was no way she was going to be left behind or be grabbed from behind and her brother didn't notice.

"Cat, seriously, I promise you I'll know if something grabs you from behind," Zac assured her. "Believe me, two minutes with you and they'd soon put you back."

"Very funny." Cat bit him on the leg.

"Ow!" Zac tried to turn around and glare at her, but he hit his head making Cat giggle. "Are you crazy?" He hissed.

"Sorry, but you were being mean," Cat told him.

"Look, up ahead," Zac told her.

"I can't see past you," Cat told him. "What is up ahead?"

"A big opening and it's sparkling with light." Zac started to crawl faster.

"Hey, wait up," Cat hissed. "I'm not as long as you are."

"Then stop chattering and hurry up," Zac told her.

Zac slid down a small lip at the end of the tunnel and Cat did the same, landing on him in a big heap.

"Geez, Cat." Zac unraveled himself from the heap of arms and legs Cat tangled them into. "You could've waited for me to have cleared the area."

"Nope, I wasn't sticking around in that hole on my own," Cat told him.

"I see you two finally figured it out," Callum's voice boomed over them. "I knew the two of you could do it if you worked together." He looked down at his teenagers. "Remember all the lessons you learned today. The most important one being..." He waited for them to answer.

"Don't trust your father because he'll get up and leave you to be eaten by the mountain goats." Cat lay on her back looking up at her father.

Zac stood up and pulled his lazy sister onto her feet.

"That when we work together, we can accomplish anything," Zac answered correctly.

"Sure." Cat's eyes narrowed accusingly at her brother before looking at her father. "What he said."

Cat looked around the cavern and her breath caught in her throat. "Oh wow," she breathed. "Are those crystals in the rocks?" Cat looked up at the jewels sending rows of red down into the cavern.

"Something like that," Callum told her. "Now we need to move so we make it through the other side in time to get to the cabin before night falls."

"Are you going to take off and leave us again?" Cat looked at him distrustfully. "Because seriously, I was about to report you to child protective services."

"You are so dramatic, my little love." Callum mussed the top of her hair, laughing at her. "Now come on, I promise no more disappearing acts." He stopped and eyed both of them sternly. "Unless you start bickering again."

"Is that a threat?" Cat challenged her father.

"No, my little darling smart mouth, that's a promise." Callum kissed her on the cheek. "Now let's get moving. Your packs are over there."

"Great." Cat sighed and scooped up her pack before plodding after her father.

They walked through the most amazing cave for just under an hour before popping out the other side of the mountain to the most breathtaking view.

"Wow!" Cat breathed.

"Yes, I agree with your 'wow'." Her father put an arm around her while the three of them stood admiring the view. "Every time your mother and I came up here we'd stop for a while and just sit quietly enjoying the view."

"It makes you feel so small, really," Zac said.

"That it does, son," Callum agreed. "I would love to stay here and take it in with my kids, but we've still got about a half an hour hike down the mountain to the cabin."

"Great!" Cat shook her head. "Then tomorrow we have to do this all over again to get home." She looked at her father and followed him when he took off down a path. "Can't we hike home from this mysterious cabin?"

"You're so lazy," Zac said to her. "Come on." He dragged her with him. "We'll walk for half an hour then when we're off the mountain you can get on my back."

"Really?" Cat looked at him thankfully.

"Yes, lazy bones." Zac laughed at her as they picked up their pace to catch their father.

Chapter Thirteen

KEEPING SECRETS

PRESENT DAY

Something startled Cat and her eyes flew open to find she'd fallen asleep with her head on her father's desk. She sat up straight and found a piece of paper stuck to her cheek. Cat didn't remember any papers on the desk when she'd sat down. A shiver crept up her spine. She pulled the paper off her face and found it was a foreclosure notice for Mountain Rise Ranch.

Cat frowned as she read the notice. A lot of people had told her how badly Chelsea was struggling but Cat didn't realize it was this bad. Images of her trip to the mountain with her father and brother were still fresh in her mind after reliving them in a very real dream. Cat shivered once again and saw that the flashlight was on and pointing up to the ceiling.

"I thought I switched that off." Cat's frown deepened as she gave the object a sideways glance. "I probably didn't though."

Another chill crept up her spine, but she looked up while she was sitting in the chair and that's when she saw it. You had to be sitting in the spot she was sitting in to see it. But it showed where the path to the rock opening was. Of course, this map must've been drawn over forty years ago now, but the mountains didn't move. Cat knew that the Cupids Bow landscape hadn't changed all that much either.

Another conversation from her eighteenth birthday supper with her father flashed through her mind. It was after he'd given her the necklace.

Remember Kitty Cat, everything you need to know is up! If you keep in mind everything you've been taught, you'll find the path as easy as pie.

Cat had thought he'd been talking about her following her own path in life and becoming a country singer. She idly fiddled with her necklace once again. But now she was thinking that was not what he'd meant at all. Everything in his sentence was a clue pointing her to the cabin on the other side of the mountain. She hadn't even remembered that cabin. Her eyes widened. What if that's where he'd stashed the trunks?

Cat stood up, a plan formulating in her mind. She knew exactly what she needed to do and who was going to help her do it. Cat's eyes narrowed as a smile lifted her lips. She picked up the envelope full of evidence against David. It was retribution time, and Cat wasn't waiting until he'd fully recovered. There wasn't time, and both his limbs seemed to be working just fine.

"Cat?" David smiled when he answered the door to his house to see her standing on his doorstep.

"Can I come in?" Cat asked him.

"Of course," David stepped back and let her enter his house. "Please excuse the mess; the cleaning crew is due tomorrow."

"I'm not here for the hospitality." Cat turned and looked at him. She was clutching her large purse. "Can we sit down?"

"Why do I have a feeling this is not a social call?" David's eyes narrowed suspiciously.

"I thought we'd already established that it's not." Cat raised her eyebrows and took a seat on a big armchair before being invited to.

"Fair enough," David said down on the sofa opposite her. "I take it you don't want any refreshments?"

"No, thank you." Cat shook her head. "What I'm after are answers and the truth."

David gave a soft laugh, and closed his eyes for a moment, shaking his head, before looking at her again. "You've been speaking to Wallace Black."

"As a matter of fact, I have," Cat confirmed. "It was a very interesting conversation as well."

"Look, Cat ..." David was about to explain but she cut him off coldly.

"I don't want to hear excuses, David," Cat told him bluntly. "Before you try to weave the truth to your benefit, I've done my own research and confirmed all the information Wallace gave me."

"I feel like I've been tried and judged here without a fair trial or even being present," David sat back and looked at her.

"I would never do that," Cat told him honestly. "But all the evidence against you, David, tells me that you're in the middle of all the trouble going on in the area."

"Things aren't what they seem on paper, Cat." David's eyes became guarded.

"My father used to say something along the same lines," Cat told him. "So, let me tell you what I know about you and the conclusion I've drawn as to why you are here."

"Okay." David nodded. "Let's hear what you've got."

"Your mother died when you were a few months old. You were raised alongside your older half-brother by your father," Cat began. "You already told me that part. But what you left out was who your mother was."

"Because I knew if I told you I would get this exact reaction from you," David pointed out.

"What am I supposed to think, David?" Cat asked him.

"Maybe ask me instead of accuse me," David told her. "That would go a long way."

"I don't have time for the long way, David," Cat told him.

"You keep saying that." David's brow creased. "That you don't have time."

"That's because I don't." Cat shook her head. "So, we need to cut through all the nonsense and cut to the chase."

"Fine," David nodded. "You know who my mother is, which means you also know who my grandfather is."

"I also know who your father is, and I now know how Zac came to have Monarch," Cat told him. "It was your father who sold Zac his Akhal-Teke."

"Yes," David nodded. "I also helped Liam with the design of the stables to model them off my father's because Zac and Jamie really liked them"

"Does Zac know who you are?" Cat asked him, staring at him intently.

"He knows who my father is," David told her. "As the only woman I ever knew as my mother was my step-mother, Zac was introduced to her as my mom."

"You never saw fit to tell him who your mother was?" Cat asked David.

"It never came up," David told her.

"With all this trouble going on, you never once thought to tell my brother who you were or your connection to the trouble." Cat's eyes narrowed. "Do you make a habit of deceiving your friends, David?"

"That's unfair," David told her. "I've never deceived Zac."

"Really?" Cat pulled a face, reached into her purse, and pulled out some papers that she dumped on the coffee table in front of him. "Do you recognize these?"

David just looked at the papers on the table.

"What?" Cat looked at him expectantly. "You've got nothing to say for yourself?"

"There's nothing to say." David looked at her blankly. "Like I said, you've obviously made up your mind about what's going on. Nothing I say is going to change that."

"Why don't you at least try?" Cat sat back and folded her arms. "I'm giving you the opportunity to try."

Their eyes locked and held. Cat felt that familiar pull like she had been drawn to him by a force stronger than herself. Her heart started to pick up a few beats and her breath caught in her throat she had to force herself to look away.

"Cat, I'm not at Cupids Bow Ranch to cause any trouble, and I never have been," David assured her. "I came here to try and alleviate it."

"Why do I find that hard to believe?" Cat looked at him curiously.

"Because you found out who I am and have painted me with the same brush as my relatives," David guessed. "Which is also unfair as you don't know my relatives either. You've all judged them on the ones you've had the misfortune to have dealings with."

"Do you realize that your grandfather started this whole thing by using his wealth and power to force my father's fiancée to marry his son?" Cat pointed out.

"I'm aware of what everyone thinks my grandfather did," David admitted. "But your father didn't help matters by stealing my uncle's bride and running away."

"We could sit here for hours arguing about who really stole whose bride," Cat told him. "But the fact of the matter is my father was dating the woman who became my mother long before your grandfather and family came to town."

"My grandfather arrived here with the sole purpose of doing business with your grandfather and father," David explained. "But they weren't interested in doing business with my grandfather."

"What business?" Cat's eyes narrowed suspiciously.

"You don't know the history of how my grandfather came to this area?" David seemed surprised.

"Let's say I don't, and you enlighten me," Cat said.

"My grandfather on my mother's side was a powerful man." David began telling Cat his family's history. "He was from a wealthy family who had connections in high places."

"Yes, I know all that," Cat nodded. "The man's children loved to lord it all over town, according to my father."

"Once again, that's pure speculation. My mother and her second youngest sister were wonderful people." David defended his family, well, part of them at least. "My grandfather was also a collector of rare antiquities. Rare jewelry pieces in particular. He had some impressive pieces of art, jewelry, and other items in his collection," David told her. "He was well known all over the world for his collection. Galleries were forever borrowing pieces for various exhibits."

"Oh," Cat looked at David, surprised. "I didn't know that."

"There was one piece in particular my grandfather was very proud of," David told her. "It was an ancient piece called the heart of Isis."

"Never heard of it." Cat made a mental note to look it up.

"It was said to be one of his most exquisite and oldest pieces of jewelry. The stone dated back to the Egyptians." David adjusted the sling on his arm.

"It must've been amazing," Cat said.

"I never saw it myself, but I believe so," David continued the story. "It was on display at one of the London museums when it was stolen."

"No way." Cat's eyes widened. "That was rather brazen of the thief."

"He was caught," David assured her. "There was no way my grandfather would let a priceless piece like that out of his grasp."

"Good for your grandfather. I don't understand what this had to do with the vendetta your grandfather had against my family though?" Cat looked at him questioningly.

"It was your father that had stolen the piece," David shocked her by saying.

"No way!" Cat shook her head in disbelief. "My father would

never steal anything. He was most certainly not a cat burglar that broke into museums."

Then suddenly it dawned on her which piece he might be referring to. Her heart started to pound in her chest. Cat had to stop herself from clutching at the pendant nestled beneath her cowgirl shirt. A story her grandmother had once told her about the pendant now hanging around her neck came back to her.

"I can prove it to you. I have all the reports and evidence backing up my story," David assured her.

"But my father has no criminal records," Cat pointed out. "Your grandfather was obviously lying for some reason. Maybe it was your grandfather that had stolen the piece from my family."

"Apparently, the British police drew the same conclusion that you just did," David surprised her by saying. "Your grandmother had filed a report with them a year before that, when she was visiting her sister in England. That was around the time my grandfather acquired the piece." He shook his head. "When your father showed up at the museum with his evidence and lawyer the museum immediately retracted the piece. They then had it tested and found out that it was not the Heart of Isis."

"Shouldn't they have done that in the first place?" Cat shook her head. "I mean how can you show something like that without having it authenticated first?"

"They had no reason to disbelieve my grandfather, who had all the papers to prove the piece was legitimate," David told her. "He'd bought it at a private auction hosted by a well-known antiquities dealer who was reputed to be able to get the rarest pieces."

"He sounds like a con man to me," Cat pointed out.

"Turns out he was." David rubbed his face.

"Surely your grandfather and other dealers must've known something was up with the dealer." Cat couldn't believe that collectors wouldn't test the items themselves or have them authenticated before even bidding on them.

"The dealer set himself up with a few real, rare pieces to begin his business," David told her.

"Reel in the big fish with prized bait and then use the cheap stuff made to look like the bait to keep them baited," Cat guessed. "I hope he's no longer operating."

"No, he's not. That ordeal nearly ruined my grandfather, Cat. It tarnished his reputation, and his entire collection came under scrutiny. Luckily the other pieces of his collection weren't acquired through that dealer." David's eyes flashed. "The first and last time my grandfather had used that particular dealer was to get the Heart of Isis. His father nearly disowned him over the stink it caused. My grandfather was pushed out of the main family business. My great-grandfather made him take over the construction side of the family business."

"Oh, so he was downgraded from running a billion-dollar business to running a multi-million dollar business." Cat's voice held not one hint of sympathy. "Some people work their whole life to be able to run a company that just turns a decent profit."

"I'm getting so tired of people demonizing owners of big corporations," David told her. "Most of them struggle and scrape their way to the top. Working darn hard to get to where they are."

"Says the owner of a multi-million dollar company that was handed down to him," Cat told him smugly. "Yes, I know that you inherited your grandfather's business and then you built it into an even bigger empire."

"I no longer run that company," David told her honestly. "It wasn't a multimillion dollar company when I took it over. In fact, most of my grandfather's family wealth had dried up a long time ago. It turns out that my great-grandfather made the worst mistake by appointing his youngest son to take over from my grandfather."

"So why did he come here then? Other than to get payback from my family for a jewel your grandfather owned illegally?" Cat's voice dripped with disdain for David's family.

"He wanted to buy that piece of jewelry from your family as it had a rare stone in it that was also very old." David fidgeted with the sling on his arm. "But your family refused to sell it. Your father was adamant that the jewel remained in the Sparrow family."

"My father's family were very loyal to this land and had a lot of superstitions about it." Cat pointed out. "You've known Zac for long enough by now to know he shares those beliefs."

"I know, and I can respect that," David admitted. "There's a lot of mystery surrounding this ranch and the land around it."

"So, this vendetta your family has against mine is over a jewel?" Cat said in disbelief.

"A priceless jewel, but no, I don't believe the troubles on the ranches stem from that," David told her. "According to my grandfather, he backed off trying to pressure your family into selling the jewel to him. He said he understood why the Sparrows wanted it kept in their family."

"He had a funny way of showing his understanding," Cat pointed out. "He's spent most of his adult life trying to destroy us and everyone around us."

"No, he didn't!" David was getting exasperated by her continued attack on his grandfather and refusing to hear or believe anything he said. "But I think my great-uncle, his younger brother, did."

"Why would he come after my family?" Cat asked David.

"At first I think it was because he was after my grandfather's antiquities," David said. "But when he couldn't get his hand on those he came after the people who he found out were hiding them for my grandfather."

"Hiding them?" Cat was surprised by that.

"Well, the collection suddenly vanished overnight." David fidgeted with the sling once again. "The same night that my great-uncle arrived to confiscate it from my grandfather. He said that the collection was bought with company funds and therefore belonged to the company." His eyes flashed with anger. "But that wasn't true, the man had falsified documents once again. He was notorious for doing that."

David's grandfather's jewels had vanished overnight, just like her family's valuable items had, Cat thought. Then another thought hit her. What if David was right and her father had hidden the antiquities collection in the same place?

"Maybe your grandfather hid it on his ranch?" Cat suggested.

"No." David shook his head. "My great-uncle found evidence suggesting the antiquities were hidden on Cupids Bow Ranch by your father."

"You think your grandfather hid his rare antiquities collection on Cupid's Bow?" Cat looked at him in amazement. "Or are you accusing my father of stealing the entire collection?"

"No, I never said your father stole the collection!" David shook his head in exasperation. "I am saying that he helped my grandfather hide them."

"First you tell me that our families aren't the mortal enemies we've known them to be," Cat reiterated. "Now you are trying to tell me that my father stashed your grandfather's valuables away." She shook her head. "What evidence did your great-uncle have to back up his claim?"

"The night my great-uncle arrived on the ranch he wasn't feeling well so he went to bed early," David told her the story. "In the early hours of the morning, he heard my grandfather talking to your father outside the house. He couldn't hear what they were saying and looked out of his bedroom window. There was a large moving truck that your father then took off in."

"Maybe he was bringing something to your grandfather," Cat suggested.

"The next morning, the collection that had been there the night before was gone." David rubbed his face.

"So, your great-uncle deduced from seeing my father with a big truck that he'd taken the antiquities?" Cat's brows raised up. "That's his evidence?"

"It was suspicious," David pointed out.

"Yes, but there could've been anything in that truck," Cat said. "Even a horse."

"I doubt it," David said. "My great-uncle was furious and tried to take away the development and construction company from my grandfather when he found that he couldn't do that because it belonged solely to my grandfather. He'd bought it from his father and severed all its connection with the parent company."

"That must've been a low blow, especially when your great-uncle needed a cash injection for the business," Cat stated.

"He snapped at that point," David told her. "My great-uncle was deep in debt and had ruined the business. Their father had a heart attack and passed away, which was yet another blow to my great-uncle because a few weeks before he died, the will was changed."

"Let me guess, your great-grandfather cut his youngest son out of the will and left everything to your grandfather?" Cat guessed correctly.

"Unfortunately for my grandfather, that meant a failing company was too far gone for him to bail out, so he sold it." David moved his position on the sofa. Cat could see he was uncomfortable. "My great-uncle became desperate. His wife left him and that was the last straw."

"So, he turned his rage onto my family?" Cat shook her head.

"He wanted my grandfather's collection at whatever cost," David told her. "He approached your family and tried to get them to hand over the collection. But your father told him he had no idea about any priceless antique collection."

"Are you trying to tell me that this trouble started way back then?" Cat's brow creased.

"Pretty much," David confirmed Cat's suspicions. "My grandfather took pity on his youngest brother and gave him a place to stay on the ranch. He also gave my great-uncle a job on the ranch."

"Why do I get the feeling that was a huge mistake on your grandfather's part?" Cat asked.

"Because it was." David nodded. "Apparently my great-uncle was a master manipulator."

"Sorry I know he's your family, but what a creep!" Cat shuddered. "I've met my fair share of people like that."

"He was able to get into my grandfather's oldest son's head,"

David explained. "Together they came up with a plan to destroy your father and his family. I think he also wanted to get his hands on that family heirloom of yours. There had been rumors that your father had given the jewel to his fiancé."

"Oh, is that why he went after my mother?" Cat's eyes widened with realization. "He thought that he'd get his hands on it that way?"

"I believe so," David told her. "There were also rumors of a great treasure hidden in a part of the Big Snowy Mountain. The part that bordered Cupids Bow Ranch."

"I've never heard about any treasure hidden in those mountains," Cat lied.

"When my great-uncle couldn't get your family to cooperate, he went after another family that was close to yours." David rested one ankle on his knee.

"It wasn't your grandfather that manipulated my mother's father into forcing her to marry his oldest son!" The truth dawned on Cat.

"No, it was his younger brother," David confirmed Cat's suspicions. "Of course, my uncle didn't mind. Rumor had it that he was infatuated with your mother."

"Yes, that much I do know from my mother's journals, along with the hell he put her through during the month they were married," Cat told him.

"My grandfather was trying to get his son to annul the marriage, but he refused; he didn't even care when my father cut him off," David told her. "Then your father and your mother decided to take matters into their own hands. They ran away together."

"Can you blame them?" Cat shook her head.

"My mother had just had me, but she came back to the ranch to talk some sense into my uncle who was also her twin brother," David explained. "My uncle tricked her into telling him where your father and mother were hiding. My uncle, mother, and great-uncle were heading to find them when their car was hit by a drunk driver."

"All three of them died in that accident," Cat's voice dropped. "I'm sorry about your mother, David."

"She was only trying to help her friend out." David's voice was filled with emotion. "You do know your mother and my mother were best friends?"

"No, I didn't know that," Cat said. "I only knew Aunt Holly."

"Your mother and Holly were bridesmaids at her wedding to my father," David shocked her by saying. "I have the pictures. My father made sure I knew who she was while I grew up."

"Wait!" Cat's eyes widened. "Was her name Penny?"

"Yes, Penny Miller." David smiled. "Why?"

"My mother has a photo album and a woman named Penny appears in a lot of them alongside her and Aunt Holly," Cat told him. "When I find it, I'll show you."

"I'd like that." David smiled.

"Did you befriend Zac to get access to Cupids Bow Ranch?" Cat swung the conversation away from their mothers so fast she saw she'd taken him by surprise.

David's eyes widened with shock at her question.

"Why on earth would you think that?" David asked her and was clearly offended by the question.

"You appeared in my brother's life at my father's wake, claiming to be one of Zac's best friends," Cat pointed out. "After hearing your story, I have to wonder."

"No," David shook his head. "I met Zac years before we ran into each other at college."

"Where?" Cat asked him, seeing his frown. "Where did you meet my brother?"

"At one of his school dances," David told her. "I was accompanying a friend of my grandfather's daughter."

"And what? You just hit it off as instant best friends?" Cat asked suspiciously.

"No, the day after the dance, Zac, his prom date, me, and my prom date all met to go riding," David told her. "Zac and I found out we were going to the same university. As neither of us knew anyone in the town we were going to, we managed to get a dorm together."

"Then you served in the army together." Cat went over David and Zac's history as friends.

"We did," David confirmed.

"Why did you set up the previous foreman of Cupids Bow Ranch to get this job, David?" Cat's eyes narrowed on him. She knew she'd once again thrown him by her sudden change of conversation. "Was it to look for your grandfather's hidden treasure? Or because you want to force us all off our land because you think there's treasure in the mountains?"

"Cat, whatever I answer, you're not going to believe me." David sighed. "Like I said before, you had already tried and convicted me before you came to see me."

"You've given me nothing to make me think differently," Cat told him. "All I know is since you and your family showed up in the area, we've had nothing but trouble."

"Cat, I'm not here to cause trouble or try to steal yours or anyone else's land," David tried to assure her. "One of the reasons I took this job was to try and stop the trouble."

"One of the reasons?" Cat looked at him with raised eyebrows.

"The other was to look for my grandfather's antiquity collection," David admitted. "But not for the reasons you think."

"I want to believe you, David," Cat told him. "But if what you say is true, why keep what you're up to or your identity a secret from Zac and all the other ranches you claim to want to help?"

"Because of the way you've just reacted to finding out who my family is," David told her. "My question to you is, why didn't you go straight to Zac with all this information?"

"Because I need your help," Cat told him.

"And you thought hanging a secret over my head would force me to help you?" David looked at her amazed.

"No," Cat denied. "Because I didn't want Zac to kick you off the land or spread the word about you before you helped me."

"Ah." David nodded. "What's stopping me from going to confess all this to Zac instead of helping you?"

"Because you want to find your grandfather's treasure," Cat told him smugly, watching his eyes widen in surprise.

"You knew about the treasure all along, yet you let me ramble on about it?" David's brows creased.

"No." Cat shook her head. "This is the first I've heard about it."

"Then how do you know where it is?" David's eyes narrowed suspiciously.

"Because my father has a secret hiding place," Cat told him. "So, all your snooping around this and the four other ranches over the years were all in vain."

"Where's this secret hiding place if not on any of the ranches?" David asked her curiously.

"Seriously?" Cat shook her head. "You think I'm going to answer that?"

"Of course not." David shook his head. "So, what do I have to do to be let in on the secret?"

Cat grinned, "I thought you'd never ask."

EPILOGUE

"I'm telling you, Cat, this is a bad idea," David hissed. "She's a very proud woman. You don't think Zac and I have tried to help her over the years?" He shook his head. "She won't even let her children help her."

"Trust me, she's in no position to refuse right now," Cat told him.

"Maybe we should start with Big Valley Ranch," David suggested.

"No!" Cat shook her head and before he could say another word, she rang the doorbell.

They heard it echo through the entrance hall. When it died down there was nothing but silence coming from the house.

"She's not home." David tilted his head and peaked into the window.

Cat turned to look at them, catching the frown on his face.

"What is it?" Cat said.

"I just saw her rush into one of the rooms." David looked at Cat. "She looked like she was in a panic."

"Maybe she thinks we're debt collectors?" Cat said.

"No, I don't think it was that." David's frown deepened.

Before Cat could stop him, he opened the door and stepped into the entry hall.

"Hello?" David called. "It's David; I'm just checking if you're okay."

David walked cautiously into the house towards the room he'd seen the owner of the house rush into. Cat followed behind him just in case they were shot at again. He stopped so suddenly in the doorway that Cat walked into him.

"Please," Cat heard the woman say. "Please can you help me?"

David didn't hesitate. He shot into the room, making Cat freeze at the scene in front of her. Chelsea Hitchin's cheeks were stained with tears, her eyes were puffy and red from crying.

"She won't wake up!" Chelsea's voice was hoarse with emotion and panic. "Please make her wake up."

Cat's eyes moved to the bed where Chelsea's mother, Debbie Hitchin, lay still and pale on the bed. The heart monitor that was attached to Debbie was beeping that terrible flat line noise Cat knew well, and it made her blood run cold. Memories of her mother in a similar condition flashed through Cat's mind and tears sprang to her eyes. But this time, they weren't tears for her loss but for what Chelsea was going through right now. Cat knew that shock, fear, and abject panic that was rushing through Chelsea's veins.

Cat swallowed and rushed to Chelsea's side so David could move over Debbie and check for a pulse, which they both knew wouldn't be there. But that deep-seated hope at the root of the fear and panic made you try anyway. Chelsea's tear-filled eyes looked up at Cat as Cat put her arm around Chelsea's shoulders.

"Please, help my mom, Cat," Chelsea's voice caught, and the tears pushed up over her eyelids before she collapsed into Cat's arms, sobbing. "I'm not ready for her to go."

"I know," Cat said softly, her own tears sliding down her cheeks as she held Chelsea and stroked her hair soothingly. "David is calling an ambulance. We'll sit with her until they get here so she's not alone."

"I only went to fill up her water," Chelsea sobbed into Cat's chest. "I wasn't even gone for five minutes. I should have never left her."

"No, Chelsea, this is not your fault," Cat soothed.

Cat held Chelsea and let her sob, while she clutched her mother's cold hand. David let the ambulance crew in, and they worked around the two of them. They even left Chelsea holding her mother's hand until they were ready to take Debbie away.

"I'm sorry, Miss Hitchin," the paramedic said softly. "But we have to take your mother now."

Chelsea raised her head, wiped her eyes, and nodded. She stood up and kissed her mother's forehead, "Goodbye mommy, I love you so much." A tear slid down her face and dotted Debbie's forehead.

The paramedic gently covered Debbie's face before rolling her out of the room. Chelsea and Cat followed them to the front door while David took point and sorted out all the details. The two of them stood watching through the front door as the ambulance pulled off before Chelsea collapsed in a heap on the floor and started to sob once more. Cat knew there was nothing she could do to take away the grief or pain Chelsea was going through. What she could do was sit on the floor next to her and give her comfort while she grieved and a strength to draw from. Cat sat down and put her arms around Chelsea, pulling her into her lap and letting her cry, while Cat's tears spilled quietly above her.

David walked back into the house and pulled the front door closed behind him. He disappeared for a few minutes. David came back with two large cushions and a blanket. He gently put the blanket around Chelsea's shoulder before surprising Cat by sitting down behind her and pulling her into his arms to support them both. Cat turned and gave him a watery, grateful smile. Then she leaned back against him, accepting his support, and warm comfort.

Cat knew at that moment without a shadow of a doubt that her father had somehow had a hand in pushing her to where she was right now. He'd always told her that forgiving someone was not for their sake but for yours. It's where the healing started. Cat swallowed down the lump in her throat and gave in to the feelings bubbling up inside her. It was time to mend an old bridge that should've been mended years ago. Seeing yet another life pass on made Cat once again remember just how short and fragile life was. You never knew what tomorrow had in store for you. All the certainty you had was here and now.

"Cat?" Chelsea said softly.

"I'm here," Cat said.

"Will you stay for a while?" Chelsea asked her.

"I'm not going anywhere," Cat promised her. "David and I are here to help with whatever we can."

"Thank you." Chelsea gave Cat a squeeze before letting the tears flow again.

Cat wasn't sure how long they sat in the entry hall like that, but Chelsea finally cried herself to sleep. David gently lifted her and took her through to the living room, where he lay her on the sofa while Cat covered her with the blanket.

"I'll call Hayden and Jamie," Cat told him.

"I'll call Zac," David offered.

It didn't take long for Jamie and Hayden, Chelsea's grown up children, to get to the ranch. By the time David and Cat left the ranch, promising to return the following day, it was late.

"Thank you, for everything today," Cat said to David as they drove to Big Valley Ranch.

"You know, Cat," David pulled to a stop outside the ranch and turned towards her, "you never had to coerce me to help you. All you had to do was ask." Their eyes met and held.

"I'm beginning to realize that." Cat smiled at him. "But I've been having big trust issues lately."

"I can understand that after everything you've been through," David told her. "But I'm nothing like either of your ex-husbands. I'd like to have the chance to prove it."

"What are you saying?" Cat's eyes narrowed and her heart

was starting to do that weird dance it always did when their eyes locked.

"Cat, I've been crazy about you since the day we met when you were eighteen," David's voice was soft and filled with feeling. "I never thought we could ever be together because we moved in different worlds. I know I'm on shaky ground with you right now, but I'm going to do everything I can to prove to you that I am worthy of your trust."

Cat sat staring at him with her heart pounding and those fluttery things inside her belly going crazy. She couldn't find her voice at that moment, and her throat had gone dry. David reached over and took her hand, which he lifted to her mouth to place a gentle kiss on her palm. He closed her fingers over it.

"That is my token of how I feel about you." David smiled at her. "I know we have a lot of work ahead of us if we're going to put your plan to save all five ranches into action. I want you to know I'm going to be right by your side every step of the way." He held onto her closed hand. "Maybe by the end of all this, I'll prove worthy of your love too."

THE SERIES CONTINUES

ARE YOU READY TO READ Mountain Rise Ranch, book 2 of the Montana Country Inn Romance Series?

To read the next book in this series, go to www.amazon.com/dp/B09WN99VMR

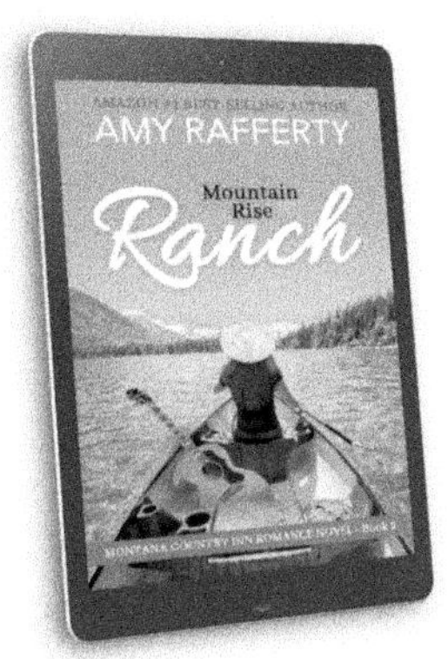
AMY RAFFERTY
Mountain
Rise
Ranch

ALSO BY AMY RAFFERTY

To dive into your next read, go to https://www.amyraffertyauthor.com/

STAY UPDATED WITH ME

Thank you so much for purchasing or downloading my book! I am grateful to all my amazing readers.

To stay updated on all my latest books, newsletters, freebies and beautiful photos from the fabulous locations I write about, why not join my VIP group?

I will send you regular pictures of La Jolla Cove, San Diego and the Florida Gulf Beaches where I try to spend as much time as I can. I live in San Diego, my own 'Garden Of Eden' and I am in love with the sea and the beaches in the area. They inspire me to write lots of beachy mystery romance fiction to share with my awesome readers like you. To join me go to https://landing.mailerlite.com/webforms/landing/y6w2d2

You will be asked for your email. You also get a FREE BOOK whenever you sign-up!

FREE BOOK

To get your FREE copy of Cody Bay Inn Prequel - Nantucket Calling go to www.amazon.com/B0992NFTY1

ABOUT THE AUTHOR

Amazon #1 Best-Seller, Amy Rafferty is a contemporary romance author of feel-good beach romance reads with heartwarming stories embracing humor and love.

Born in New York, previously a Lawyer, she now lives in San Diego with her beautiful children and cats!

Aside from writing, publishing and running her home, she spends as much time as she can visiting the beautiful San Diego and Florida beaches where she has family and friends. She calls San Diego her 'Garden of Eden', inspiring her to write clean and wholesome romance novels incorporating mystery, suspense and adventures for her characters as they find a way to open their hearts and let true love in.

facebook.com/amyraffertyauthor

instagram.com/amyraffertyauthor

www.ingramcontent.com/pod-product-compliance
Ingram Content Group UK Ltd.
Pitfield, Milton Keynes, MK11 3LW, UK
UKHW021700190726
13853UKWH00001B/384